STEAL AWAY

STEAL AWAY

V. M. BURNS

W♦RLDWIDE

TORONTO • NEW YORK • LONDON
AMSTERDAM • PARIS • SYDNEY • HAMBURG
STOCKHOLM • ATHENS • TOKYO • MILAN
MADRID • WARSAW • BUDAPEST • AUCKLAND

*This book is dedicated to Mrs. Ella Bethany,
the inspiration for Mama B.*

WORLDWIDE™

ISBN-13: 978-1-335-90146-0

Steal Away

First published in 2020 by Camel Press,
an imprint of Epicenter Press, Inc.
This edition published in 2024.

Copyright © 2020 by V.M. Burns

Recycling programs
for this product may
not exist in your area.

Harlequin Enterprises ULC
22 Adelaide St. West, 41st Floor
Toronto, Ontario M5H 4E3, Canada
www.ReaderService.com

Printed in U.S.A.

ACKNOWLEDGMENTS

Thanks to Jennifer McCord at Camel Press and Dawn Dowdle at Blue Ridge Literary Agency for all of your help, patience and understanding.

Thanks to Adrena Bethany for the banana pudding recipe and my sister, Jackie Rucker, for the Dressing recipe.

Thanks to my tribe, especially Matt O'Dwyer, Patricia Lillie and Jeff Evans, for help with character names. Thanks to my work family and to my friends Shelitha and Sophia for all of your encouragement and support.

Steal away, steal away,
Steal away to Jesus
Steal away, steal away home
I ain't got long to stay here

ONE

THE SUN BEAT down on my skin, and I was thankful I had on a T-shirt and shorts rather than my normal uniform, even though my T-shirt stuck to my chest. It was unusually hot for October in St. Joseph, Indiana, and the extra weight from my gun and the other tools on my belt added to my discomfort. On the grass by the St. Joseph River, a breeze would have been nice. Unfortunately, all we got was the hot, humid and fishy smell combined with the rotting flesh that accompanied the body we'd just fished out of the water.

"RJ, can I leave?"

Marti Alexander was a tall woman with wavy dark hair and green eyes. She was wearing a jumpsuit and boots and a bright orange vest. She had to be roasting. Beside her sat Callie, a large black standard poodle wearing an orange vest. Callie panted, despite the fact that her coat was sheared close to her body.

"Just about." I walked closer. "What made you come out today?" I tried to soften the interrogation sound in my voice by smiling. "Don't tell me you're clairvoyant."

Marti shook her head. "Someone from the St. Joseph Police Department sent me a text to come here."

I paused for a second. "You got a text message?"

"I thought it was odd. I've never gotten contacted for a search and rescue via text before." She shrugged. "I figured St. Joseph Police Department was moving into the twenty-first century."

"Do you still have it?"

She pulled her cell phone out of her pocket, made a few swipes and then handed it to me.

I read the message several times and then handed the phone back. "I'm going to need you to bring the phone into the station so we can have our tech team take a look."

Marti nodded. She was a bit shaken, but then she'd just found a man's body in the river. That's enough to shake anyone. However, this wasn't the first body Marti and her standard poodle, Callie, had found. Normally, both were granite. Today, Marti's hands shook and her eyes darted around like ping pong balls.

"Mind if I give Callie her reward?" she asked.

"Not at all." I watched as she walked across the street so that she was well away from the crime scene. She pulled a red ball out of her pocket, unclipped the leash from Callie's collar and then tossed the ball as far as she could. Callie bounded off at top speed and leaped in the air and caught the ball. Then, with a flick of her head, she tossed the ball up in the air and leapt up and caught it. She shook it several times in a way that reminded me of my godmother, Mama B, shaking dirt from a rug. Then, she dropped it, crouched down and pounced. Watching her play made me smile every time. It was her dance of joy after a find. She had earned her right to play, and she was enjoying every minute of it.

Marti and Callie were contractors who performed

search and rescue for the St. Joseph Police Department, and I'd worked with them several times in the past. Marti was related to the coroner somehow, but I wasn't exactly sure about the connection. In addition to search and rescue, Marti bred standard poodles and taught obedience classes. I'd recently bought one of her puppies for my girlfriend, Paris, so I was getting very familiar with Marti and Callie from the stories Paris shared.

After Callie had played for several minutes, Marti whistled like she was hailing a New York taxi. Callie picked up her ball and trotted back to her owner's side. Callie turned over her red ball and sat quietly while her owner reconnected her leash. Marti gave Callie a hug and several pats before she took the ball and returned it to her pocket. The two walked back to me.

"You okay?" I asked. She seemed a little groggy.

Marti looked pale, although it might have been due to the heat or the stench or exhaustion. Whatever the cause, something about her was off. The two hadn't had to track long. There was a flannel shirt left nearby. Callie sniffed it and then went to work. It wasn't long before Callie alerted her owner to the find by lying down. The body, which had drifted into a shallow area of the river that was blocked by tall brush and weeds, had been faced down, so she'd been spared the worst of it. But the smell was something that seeped into your nostrils and up into your nasal passages and refused to leave.

"I'm just hot and have a horrible headache." Marti wiped sweat from the back of her neck and took a swig from a water bottle. "Can I go?"

"Sure. Just come by the station tomorrow—ah, make it Monday morning—and finish the paperwork. Bring your phone, and we'll try to figure out where the text message came from. And don't forget Callie's card."

Callie earned points for each search she performed and bonus points for finds. I learned from Marti that the points the dog earned determined her ranking amongst other dogs doing similar work and garnered titles within the Search and Rescue Association. Each time Callie reached a new level, Marti sewed a new patch onto her orange vest. She currently had an even dozen.

I watched as they ducked under the police tape and made their way to a beat-up old Honda CRV that had seen better days. Marti wasn't the most talkative person on the best of days, but today she was even quieter than normal. Something was bothering her, but it was none of my business. I had enough problems of my own without borrowing some from anyone else.

I yawned. The nightmares I'd been struggling with for over a year were back, and I hadn't had much sleep. After a couple of months of restful sleep, my trauma induced insomnia was back with a vengeance and I was paying for it today. Nevertheless, life moved on, at least for some of us. I stared down at the body on the ground and wondered what he'd done to warrant the bullet in his head and the dip in the river.

"RJ, I think you need to see this." Detective Martinez, a new addition to the forensic team, stood near the body.

I walked over, careful to avoid a couple of empty beer bottles that were lying nearby that someone had marked with numbers, indicating they were potential evidence. The beer bottles, miscellaneous scraps of paper, candy wrappers and dirty diapers most likely had nothing to do with our murder, but we bagged and tagged everything anyway. Years on the force had taught me that nothing could be discounted as evidence, although a lifetime of living in St. Joseph, Indiana, had taught me that people enjoyed tossing their litter in the park.

I leaned over the detective's shoulder to get a better look at what he wanted to show me. Squatting wasn't something my knee would tolerate after my accident. Although getting down wasn't the problem, I wasn't about to embarrass myself in front of a junior officer by having to be helped back up like an old man. Mid-thirties wasn't old to anyone old enough to vote, but the police force had a way of relegating imperfect detectives to desk jockeys.

Detective Martinez held a wallet he'd obviously removed from the victim's pants in his gloved hands. He slid the driver's license out. I raised an eyebrow when I saw the name but said nothing. Martinez and I exchanged a glance. I stood and tried to stretch out the cramp that had just come into my neck.

I looked around for Marti, but she was already gone without explaining why the murder victim had the same last name as her ex-husband. I didn't believe in coincidences, and even if I did, this wasn't one of them. I pulled out my cell phone and swiped a few times to find Marti's number, but I stopped myself before I called. Marti Alexander wasn't a cop, but she worked with us and was related to our coroner, which meant she was connected and due a little extra courtesy than I would normally give a civilian. I took a chance that she wouldn't make a run for it and replaced my phone. She was coming in on Monday. One more day wouldn't make a major difference. Besides, Harrison is a common name. There was a chance it was a fluke. I didn't believe in flukes any more than I believed in coincidences, but I was willing to take a chance on that whole "innocent until proven guilty" stuff. The crick in my neck worked its way down my back, and before this case ended, I suspected it would settle in my posterior region. I could already tell this case was going to be a major pain in my backside.

TWO

In my African-American community, Sunday was a day for worship. This was the day we went to church, sang, praised the Lord and paid tithes and offerings. Lately, that meant the early service at First Baptist Church, FBC to the members.

I parked in the gravel lot across from the small brick building and hurried up the stairs and into the vestibule. I was running late, and the vestibule was packed with robed choir members lined up and ready to march in, along with other members who were late. Devotion was going on inside the sanctuary, and through the closed swinging doors, I heard Deacon Jenkins finishing a scripture reading, which I knew from experience would soon be followed by prayer. Devotion at FBC consisted of a song, a scripture reading, a prayer and then another song, all of which was led by members of the deacon's board. Deacons in the Baptist church were ordained men who assisted the pastor in many areas, including communion and baptism. They also handled much of the church business and finances. Some Baptist churches had female deacons, called "deaconesses," but FBC hadn't progressed to that point.

The scripture reading and prayer were sacred. The

ushers wouldn't allow the doors to be opened, which caused a backup in the vestibule. I sidled past one of the choir members and waited with the other latecomers.

"RJ."

I glanced around to see who had whispered my name. This was the third Sunday, so the young adult and children's choirs would be singing. I spotted Chris Green standing nearby.

Chris had just turned sixteen. At five foot eight, he was smaller than most of the boys his age and had a slight build, short hair and one earring. Chris and I both bore a resemblance to each other, even though I was a lot taller. We both had slender builds, dark brown eyes and skin the color of coffee with a touch of cream.

I scrutinized him carefully, but with his choir robe on, there wasn't a lot to see. Although, I was pleased that his eyes looked clear and alert.

Chris got into some trouble a few months ago. He had been hanging around the wrong crowd. Fortunately, witnessing a scary act of violence, in which a classmate nearly lost his life and a subsequent trip to the precinct were enough to scare him straight. I knew his grandmother, Sister Dorothea Green, well, and she believed I'd worked a miracle in getting her grandson back on track.

I smiled back at him. We fist bumped but didn't have time to talk. Deacon Jenkins must have finished his scripture reading and prayer because the ushers opened the doors. Those not in the choir entered.

I went into the sanctuary, turned right and looked for my godmother, Mama B. I knew she'd be in her favorite pew, fourth from the rear, and near the end. The usher standing on the right side of the building recognized me and smiled as he handed me a program and directed me to my usual seat next to Mama B.

Mrs. Ella Bethany was my godmother. She was a large, heavyset woman in her sixties. She had light skin and bright eyes. She always dressed up for church, and today's ensemble included a gold pillbox hat encased in a ribbon with a gold lamé and rhinestone-studded broach. The gold hat matched her brown and gold suit jacket that had gold thread woven through and her brown skirt. She slid down from the end of the pew to allow me to sit, and even though she never spoke, her eyes said, *You're late*.

I ignored her eyes, sat and leaned over and kissed her cheek.

At six foot three I appreciated that she slid down so I could sit on the end and extend my legs into the aisle. I wouldn't describe myself as devout, although I was raised in the church and attended nearly every Sunday for the first half of my life. Most of that time, my attendance was mandated by my parents. My dad was a deacon and my mom had been active with the Sunday School, so attendance for my sister and me was mandatory.

When the deacons finished the hymn, they took their seats on the front row, and the congregation stood as the main doors were opened. The musicians started playing, and the choir marched into the church to a rousing rendition of "Oh Happy Day" by Edwin Hawkins. I looked over and saw Chris Green near the front of the line. Sister Dorothea had done a great job raising her grandson single-handedly after her daughter Angel, Chris's mom, moved away. Angel was involved with drugs and had overdosed when Chris was a baby. So, Sister Dorothea was the only mother he had ever really known.

Watching Chris, I smiled as I reminisced. I thought back to when I was Chris's age. I went through a rebellious period where I argued, pushed back and practiced subversive acts of disobedience to avoid the two-hour weekly penance of Sunday church attendance. More than twenty years later, I remembered the final standoff. My mother sat at the kitchen table crying, while my dad, solemn and stoic, told me the requirements to live under their roof included weekly church attendance. I didn't have to like it, but I would have to endure it or move out. At sixteen, my parents' dictate felt harsh. I even remembered the emotional roller-coaster ride I took. I went from anger to sadness and hit every emotion in between. However, one look at my mother as she wept added guilt to the mix. Already dealing with hormones and the insecurities that went with being a teen, I folded like a house of cards. I slunk to my room, dressed and vowed when I left for college in a couple of years that I'd never go to Sunday school or church again.

The choir processional ended, and we went through the litany and Lord's Prayer, part of the weekly ritual. Only when the last bars of the Lord's Prayer finished was the congregation allowed to sit.

I continued to watch Chris as the young adult choir he sang in performed their first song. It was a familiar tune, and I stretched my legs into the aisle and relaxed. I was grateful for the extra legroom the aisle afforded me.

I glanced over at my girlfriend, Paris Williams, who was helping with the children's choir. Paris was one of the reasons I not only attended weekly service but now found myself coming at eight in the morning. I chuckled when I remembered my vow of never going to church or Sunday school again. I fully intended to keep that promise until college courses of chemistry, calculus and physics kicked my butt and brought me to my knees. Failing those classes meant leaving my semi-independent collegiate world and returning with my tail tucked between my legs to St. Joseph, Indiana, and my parents' rules. Desperation drove me to attend church service. In my muddled teenage mind, I somehow felt God would be more inclined to listen to my prayers and help me pass my courses if I attended church. In my heart, I knew God's blessings weren't earned, but in my head…it made perfect sense.

"Ouch."

Mama B jabbed an elbow in my ribs. "Wake up."

"I'm not sleeping," I whispered.

She raised an eyebrow and then reached into her purse and handed me a mint.

I took the mint, folded my arms and concentrated. Honestly, given the precious few hours of sleep I was getting, I would have been thankful for a nap, even at the risk of upsetting my godmother. Unfortunately, sleep was being elusive.

Rev. Hilton V. Hamilton's message was short, and the service was over in less than the ninety minutes allowed for the early service. After church, I used my superhero powers to dodge hugs and get through the crowds as quickly as possible. At six foot three, my legs allowed me to move quickly, and I used my speed to get to the parking lot. By the time Mama B arrived at the church steps, I had the car waiting out front.

She looked up, saw me and hurried down to the car. Well, hurried might be an exaggeration, but she shuffled along at a reasonable pace.

I got out and held the door for her, and once she was safely tucked inside, I got behind the wheel. In less than two minutes, we were at her front door, and that's not an exaggeration. I timed it. Mama B lived down an alley about two blocks from the church. The alley used to be lined with houses, but these had all either burned or fallen down. Those that remained were boarded up. Despite the fact that there was very little traffic, I didn't like the idea of her walking down that alley, especially at night. There were no streetlights, and it looked like the perfect setting for a murder. However, even though Mama B lived in 'the hood,' she was probably safer than the mayor.

As a cop, I should have been concerned for Mama B living in that neighborhood. I would have been worried for anyone else who lived there, but Mama B had talked to, fed, encouraged and reprimanded with love every thug, gang banger and hoodlum in the area, and I knew they had declared her Switzerland, neutral. Anyone who so much as looked cross-eyed at her would find themselves attacked from all sides. Her status meant that not only did she walk through that alley unmolested, but she left her doors unlocked most of the times, something that made my heart skip beats. She attributed the fact that she had never been burglarized to the fact that she *ain't got nothing worth stealing.* However, I knew a drug-crazed junkie looking for something to hock wouldn't care if her television was the old-fashioned type with tubes and antennas or a flat panel and thin as a razor and the size of a Buick. Anyone intent on stealing would find something to hock, even if it meant tearing the electric wires out of the wall to strip the copper. Nevertheless, she remained safe, year after year. Perhaps even drug-crazed thugs had moments of rational thought or self-preservation.

Mama B's house sat at the end of the second alley and across from the back of the southeast side recreation center. The center was a single-story brick building, and the concrete basketball court had two poles with bare rims. However, the lack of netting didn't stop the games. High school stars with NBA dreams played ball at the center nearly every day until the snow piled up too high in the winter. Mama B and her guests watched games that rivaled anything played at Madison Square Garden right from the comfort of her front porch. The weather was warm, and there were quite a few cars parked at the center, and it appeared an exciting game was underway. I went inside and got a glass of sweet tea from the kitchen and then took a seat on the front porch and watched the entertainment.

Mama B went into the house and took off her Sunday finery. When she came outside, she was wearing a cotton house dress, house shoes and a hairnet over her head. We sat in a comfortable silence for close to an hour, which was only interrupted by my commentary on the basketball game or the horns of passing cars who waved at Mama B.

Mama B didn't wear a watch, but some internal clock told her it was getting close to noon. "I got smothered cabbage and pork chops in the kitchen. Church will be over soon, and you better get a plate before folks start dropping by."

She loved to feed people, especially me, and I loved that about her.

I followed instructions and fixed my plate. Mama B's fried pork chops were one of my favorite foods, but my heart skipped a beat when I opened the refrigerator and saw that she had made a banana pudding for dessert.

By the time I finished my first plate, the yelling and trash talking coming across the alley indicated the basketball game was reaching its climax. I had no idea how they kept track of the time. I never saw anything resembling a clock. Best I could tell, they played until they were tired and wanted a break or when it got too dark to see.

By the time I finished my second helping of banana pudding, the first visitor arrived. Like Mama B and the ballers across the alley, I could guess the time without looking at my watch. That first visitor meant the second service at church was over.

Laura Leigh was a forty-something Southern maid with a soft, West Georgia accent. She was six feet tall, slender with long legs and a short afro and skin that Mama B called, "high yellow." She walked onto the porch, and I rose to give her my seat. "Hey, RJ, you don't need to get up for me."

Mama B's metal porch chair squeaked as she smiled at her guest and invited her to get a plate.

"I'll get something in a few minutes. I just need a moment to rest." She flopped down into the chair I had vacated. She turned to Mama B. "It sure is hot for October." Laura Leigh pulled out one of the small rectangular fans we called *funeral fans*. This one was a cardboard rectangle with a high-resolution serene pastural photograph of a white country chapel on one side and an advertisement for a local funeral parlor on the back. The cardboard was affixed to a wooden stick.

"The heat feels good to me," Mama B said. "You must be going through *the change*." She rocked. "You probably need the patch."

Laura Leigh laughed. "What makes you think that?"

Mama B grinned. "If it walks like a duck and talks like a duck, then it's probably a duck."

I'd listened to a lot of conversations in my time, but this was not one I wanted to think about, so I was ecstatic when I saw Paris walking down the alley. "I'm going to drive down and meet Paris." I hurried into the kitchen to put my plate in the sink. I remembered to grab the containers from the refrigerator that Mama B had prepared for me and Paris and then rushed outside. I kissed Mama B on the cheek and ignored the mischievous look in her eyes.

"You bring my good Tupperware back now, ya hear?"

"Yes, ma'am." I waved at Laura Leigh and hopped into my car. I drove down the alley and met Paris before she got to the last block.

She got into the car and gave me a kiss.

"Boy, am I glad to see you."

Paris smiled. "I would like to believe you missed me, but I suspect there's something else behind your haste." She gave me a sideways glance. "You tore out of there like a criminal escaping from prison."

I turned the car around. "You should thank me."

She raised her eyebrow. "What would I be thanking you for? I didn't even get a chance to say hello to Mama B."

"I just saved you from a conversation about menopause. They were just starting to talk about *the change of life*." I glanced away from the road to look at her face and was rewarded when I saw the relief in her eyes.

"Thank you."

"You're welcome."

Paris Williams was a tall, curvy African-American woman with dark skin like chocolate milk, gray eyes with gold flecks that sparkled when she smiled and a great smile. We've been dating for over six months, and I still felt my heart race whenever I saw her. She owned two hair salons, and her own hair looked drastically different practically every time I saw her. Today, she had her hair in a million small braids she called "microbraids." I was amazed by the versatility Black women used when it came to their hair. Regardless of how it was styled, Paris always looked great no matter how she wore her hair. Although, I might be slightly biased in my opinion.

For months, our Sunday afternoons included time spent walking at Howard Park, which was located near both of our homes. A few months ago, I gave Paris a puppy for her birthday, a black standard poodle. Now, our time at the park included Maya. The dog's official name, the one registered with the American Kennel Club, was Phoenix Still I Rise. I've learned a lot about poodles since getting this puppy for Paris. Phoenix was the name of Marti Alexander's Kennel. While Phoenix Still I Rise was the dog's registered name, it would

probably only be heard if she were shown in an AKC
dog show. It was also the name of a famous poem by
Paris's favorite author and poet, Maya Angelou, which
is where the dog's *call name* came from. The call name
was basically what a dog owner intended to "call" their
dog, like a nickname. For everyday purposes, she was
Maya. Paris had spent days trying to come up with just
the right name, and I'd listened to a lot of options before
she settled on Maya.

We stopped by Paris's house and picked up Maya
before setting out for the park, which wasn't far away
from her house. We walked around the park and practiced giving Maya the basic commands Paris had been
learning in obedience class with Marti, like SIT/COME
and DOWN. Poodles were smart dogs, but the puppies had the attention span of a gnat and were full of
energy. Mostly, Maya listened and obeyed fairly well;
however, there were days when she reminded us that
she was just a puppy, like when she pounced on leaves
and rolled around in the grass for the pure pleasure of
it. At first, I wondered how Paris would respond, but I
needn't have worried. So far, everything Maya did was
okay with Paris, which made me happy.

"How are your obedience classes going?"

Paris paused from her game of fetch. "Great. Marti's
great with dogs."

"Speaking of Marti, have you noticed anything…
different about her?" I tried to make my voice sound
neutral, but I could tell by the look Paris gave me that
she knew I was fishing for information.

She thought for a few moments. "She's not the most
talkative person I've ever met, but lately she's been qui-

eter than usual." She shrugged. "Probably normal given everything she's dealing with at the moment."

"What is she dealing with?"

She gave me a hard stare. "She's still struggling since her divorce and I don't know if there's any truth in it, but I heard she was struggling financially and actually had to sell some of her dogs."

"Who'd you hear that from?"

She took the stick from Maya and gave me another sideways glance. "I'm pretty sure I heard it from Sir Percy. He mentioned it a few weeks ago when we went to Chief Mike's birthday party."

Sir Percy was the St. Joseph Police Department's coroner, Percival Cottsworth. He was also Marti Alexander's uncle or something. Percy hadn't been knighted, but he'd picked up the title from the detectives on the force due to his British accent. He'd come to the United States on an exchange program in college years ago and never went back. He said he was too fond of warm weather and Vegas slot machines to return to the United Kingdom.

"Did he say what happened?"

"Honestly, you were standing right there when he told us about it. I knew you weren't paying attention." She sighed. "Apparently, her husband, Jake, dumped her for another woman."

I vaguely remembered the conversation but had learned to zone out any that resembled gossip unless I needed it for a case. Sir Percy was a nice man, but he was as big of a gossip as Mama B.

"I mentioned Marti looked a little…sad."

"How could you tell the difference?" I said. "She always seems sad to me."

Paris smiled. "She's not sad at dog class. When she's surrounded by dogs, she's happy." She petted Maya. "He said she had 'man trouble.' Her husband wanted a divorce so he could marry his secretary." She scowled and muttered something that sounded like *just like a man*.

I held up both hands. "Why are you giving me that look?"

She shook her head. "Sorry, it's just so unoriginal. I don't understand men who cheat."

I reached out and pulled her into my arms. "Me either." I kissed her. "My father told me a man who cheated on his wife was a weakling who deserved to be horse whipped."

She nuzzled close. "I think I would have liked your father."

I chuckled. "You would have really liked my mother. She said a man who cheated should be castrated." I felt her laughter before I heard it.

"You're right, I would have liked your mother."

We cuddled a few minutes until Maya nosed in between us. Sometimes, I wasn't sure I liked that dog. We put her leash on and walked.

"Should I ask why you're asking about Marti?" she said.

I thought about it for a few minutes. I didn't discuss active cases, but most of what I knew would be in the newspapers anyway. "Yesterday, we found a dead body in the river. According to the driver's license, it was Marti's husband, Jake."

She gasped. "Marti must be devastated. You should have told me sooner. We need to stop and pick up some food and take to her house."

"She and Callie actually found the body."

"Oh, that had to be horrible. How is she holding up?"

"No idea. She barely reacted," I said.

"Shock?" She raised an eyebrow.

I glanced away, but she wasn't having it and reached up and put both hands on either side of my face, forcing my gaze to meet hers. She then stared into my eyes and searched my soul. The examination was thorough and left no area untouched.

She shook her head. "You can't believe she did that. You can't believe she killed her husband."

"I don't know what to believe, but if he was unfaithful and left her for another woman..." I shrugged. "Less than ten percent of murder victims are killed by strangers." I paused to let that sink in. "Almost a third of all victims knew the person who killed them. There's a reason the first person we look at in a homicide investigation is the spouse. I know you don't want to believe someone you know is capable of murder, but given the right circumstances, it's possible that Marti killed her husband."

She shook her head. "No, it's not." She and Maya walked away. "Marti didn't kill her husband, and you're going to prove it."

I stood and watched for several moments. This case was definitely going to be a pain.

THREE

PARIS AND I spent the remainder of the day together and the subject of Marti Alexander never came up again. When it started to get late, I took her to get her car from the church. Since I was so close to Mama B's, I swung by one last time.

The basketball game at the rec center was still going strong. Or maybe it was a new game. It was hard to tell. There was an enthusiastic crowd of spectators, and if the noise was an indication, then the action was heating up.

Mama B wasn't on the front porch, but the front door was open. When I climbed the steps, I saw her sitting in her favorite chair, a large leather recliner. The chair was probably older than me. The leather, discolored from years of sweat and sunlight, was cracked and had molded itself to fit her frame. The front door was open and the screen unlocked, as usual.

"Come in." She didn't bother moving from her chair.

The cop in me bristled every time I came by and saw the door unlocked, but she wasn't concerned, and I knew she was safer than most of the people in town, including me. I went in, walked over and planted a kiss on her cheek.

"You didn't bring Paris with you?"

I sat on the sofa which was next to the front door. "She had Maya. She said to thank you for the food and that she'll bring your Tupperware to the Scholarship Committee Meeting."

Mama B rocked. "Why didn't you bring Paris?"

"She had the puppy with her and didn't want her to ruin your house."

"Pshaw. You tell her to come and bring her puppy. I ain't got nothing that the dog can harm." She rocked for several moments. "You tell her to come and bring that dog," she repeated.

"She isn't housebroken yet," I said. "She might have an accident on your floor."

"Ha! Most of the folks that come in here ain't housebroken." She chuckled. "You tell her to bring her puppy."

I held up both hands in surrender.

The television was tuned into a channel that played old sitcoms and dramas from the 1960s and '70s. Mama B liked wholesome shows like *Andy Griffith*, *Gomer Pyle* and *Gunsmoke*, shows with humor and no explicit sex. Some of the shows contained violence, but the good guys always won. Today, she was watching *Bonanza*.

"You can turn the channel if you want."

I shook my head. "I'm fine."

She smiled and gave me the look that said, *I know you're lying, but that's okay.* We sat in a companionable silence for several minutes. "You got something on your mind."

I had no idea how she knew when something was bothering me, but she had an uncanny radar that always picked up on my moods. She stated it as a fact, not a question, and I didn't have an answer anyway.

"You ain't sleeping."

There was no point in denying it. "I get a couple of hours, but…"

"You got something on your mind."

"Are you joking?" I laughed. "I have a lot of things on my mind."

She rocked. "You ain't gonna have no peace until you take care of your business."

"What business? I'm investigating a murder, but then I'm a cop. I investigate a lot of murders. It's what I do."

She gazed at me but didn't respond. Her silences screamed louder than any of her words.

"What?"

"I don't know what's on your mind, but I do know you're gonna need to figure it out." She returned her attention to *Bonanza* even though she'd probably seen this episode so many times she could recite the lines by heart. "When you get your business straight, then you'll have peace and you'll be able to sleep."

I waited for more. I wanted more insight, more wisdom, something, but she merely rocked and watched Ben Cartwright, played by Lorne Greene, help his sons defeat evil, run their thousand-acre ranch, the Ponderosa, and win the heart of a beautiful woman in less than one hour.

MONDAY MORNING, I arrived at the precinct bright and early, which was one advantage of not sleeping. I used to try to run, forcing my body to adapt from the surgery, but the metal plate in my knee wasn't cooperating, and I realized I was doing more harm than good and gave up. Now, I worked. My paperwork and expense reports had never been as up-to-date as they were now.

Harley arrived early too. Even though I was African American and he was Caucasian, we were alike in a lot of ways. We were both slender and over six feet tall, although at six foot three, I had more than an inch on him. At thirty-three, I was also seven years his senior. However, we hit it off from the moment we met and shared similar taste in food, movies and books. Despite the fact that Harley Wickfield the IV had been born into an affluent Southern family that reveled in their confederate heritage, he was my friend, and I not only liked him, but I trusted him.

"Good morning, want a donut?" He smiled and handed me a bag that came from my favorite bakery, Adamo's.

I took out the chocolate glazed donut he knew I liked and took a bite. "You realize you're perpetuating the stereotype about cops and donuts, right?"

He shoved a powdered donut in his mouth. "I'm okay with that."

He must have swallowed the donut because he finished it so quickly, I couldn't believe he had time to chew it. He loved powdered donuts. He whistled as he sat down and logged into his computer.

"You're in a good mood," I said and leaned forward. "If I didn't know better, I'd say you look like a man in love."

Harley chuckled. "Maybe I am."

Something in his tone caused me to look more carefully. "Mama B will be happy to hear it." I sat back in my chair. "Okay, spill it. What's her name?"

Before he could reply, my phone rang. I recognized

the coroner's number. "Hold that thought." I picked up. "Sir Percy, whaddya got for me?"

I listened for a few seconds and then hung up.

"What's up?" Harley said. "Does he have a cause of death on the corpse from the weekend?"

"He wants me to come to the morgue." I stood up. "I guess I'll find out when I get there."

We walked to the morgue together. The new Coroner's Office was in the basement of the annex across the parking lot from our office. The old office was a dank, dark closet in the basement of the station. The new office was a lot brighter, although it remained very sterile and cold.

The coroner, Percival Cottsworth, or Sir Percy as we called him, was as close to a classic picture of Santa Claus as anyone I'd ever seen. He was short, round and jovial, with piercing blue eyes, a white beard and a jelly-belly. The only deviations from Santa were the cigars he chomped when inside and lit when outside and his British accent. He came to the States on an exchange program in college and never left. He loved the weather in Florida, the casinos in Vegas and the quiet life in northwestern Indiana, which he said reminded him of home in the Kent countryside.

When we swiped our badges and entered the secure area of the morgue, we were greeted not just by Sir Percy but Marti Alexander.

I was surprised at her unexpected appearance, but Harley's reaction was more than surprise. He was stunned.

I glanced at my partner, and the glazed look in his eyes spoke volumes. I hid the smile that threatened to breakout on my face, walked forward and extended my hand. "Hi, Marti." I turned back to where Harley stood rooted to the spot, mouth open. "Have you met my partner, Harley Wickfield?"

Hearing his name must have jolted him from his stupor. Harley grinned. "We met a couple of days ago."

Marti's face looked clueless. Their meeting had obviously not been as memorable for her as it was for him.

"You remember," Harley said, "I stopped you for speeding."

Marti squinted. "I remember."

Harley stumbled over his words. "You were driving pretty fast, but I only gave you a ticket for not wearing your seat belt...remember?"

"How could I forget." She mumbled, "You're going to cost me seventy-five dollars."

Harley's face looked crestfallen. "You were driving fifty-five in a forty, that's fifteen over the speed limit." He smiled. "I could have given you reckless driving for going fifteen over the limit. But I cut you a break and only cited you for not wearing a seat belt. It doesn't put points on your license."

"You made me take a sobriety test."

Harley's face flushed red. "Well, you were acting... odd."

She took a deep breath and narrowed her eyes. "Odd? I was acting odd?" She laughed. "Maybe I was acting odd because I'd just discovered my ex-husband's dead body at the river and was trying to get home so I could puke in the peace and comfort of my own home."

Harley stopped and stared.

"Have a seat, Marti," I said and pointed to a chair in the cramped space Sir Percy used as an office.

She took a deep breath and sat.

I took a deep breath. "How come you didn't tell me the body belonged to your husband?"

"Ex-husband," Sir Percy said around the cigar dangling from his mouth.

"Okay, ex-husband. You should have told me you knew the deceased. Why didn't you?"

Marti sat for a few moments. "I don't know."

"That's not good enough." I knew I was coming across harsh, but I needed the truth.

Sir Percy gave her shoulder a pat and frowned at me. "Come on, RJ. Give the lass a break. She was upset."

Marti held up a hand. "It's okay. RJ's right." She released a heavy sigh. "I should have said something at the time, but for the life of me, I couldn't. I just couldn't acknowledge to anyone, not even myself, that Jake was dead…murdered."

Harley had composed himself and had pulled out a notepad and pen. "When's the last time you saw your *ex-husband*?"

"Friday night. He came—"

"This past Friday?" I asked.

She nodded.

I shot a glance at the coroner.

"I know what you're going to ask." He removed his cigar and picked up a file and flipped through it. "The time of death was most likely early Saturday morning. Unfortunately, that's all of the information I have. Once I saw who it was, I had to remove myself from the case." His eyes softened as he looked at Marti. "Given my connection to the deceased."

This case was getting more complicated by the minute. The person who found the body had been married to the victim. The coroner was related to victim or the suspect. I wasn't sure. I looked from Marti to Sir Percy. "How are you two related?"

"She's my niece, after a fashion. My late wife raised Marti after her parents were killed. I've known her since she was a babe."

That was just great. I turned back to Marti. "Tell me about Friday."

"There's nothing to tell. He came to the house in the middle of the night. It had to be…one o'clock. He was drunk."

"Hardly surprising," Sir Percy mumbled.

"He was looking for Carolyn, his wife. I was—"

"Excuse me," I said. "Why would your ex-husband come to *your* house looking for his wife?"

She colored and took a deep breath. "Because she left him. She'd been hiding out at my house for over a week."

"Hiding out?" Harley asked. "Was he violent?"

Marti looked nervous. "Yes…no… I don't know. He had a temper, but he'd never actually gotten violent." She looked down. "At least, not with me."

"But he drank like a fish." Sir Percy looked kindly at Marti. "He might have become violent."

"Maybe he had become violent," Marti said. "Carolyn was certainly beaten up pretty badly when she came to my house. She had a busted lip and bruises all over her body."

"Did she file a police report?" I asked, even though I knew the answer before the words left my lips.

She shook her head. "I tried to get her to file a report with the police. I even offered to come with her, but she refused."

"So, he shows up on Friday night."

"He banged on the doors and threatened to break the door down if I didn't open up so he could talk to Carolyn." She shivered. "I've never known him to get that upset before."

"What happened next?"

"I refused to open the door. I told him if he didn't go away, I'd..." She looked down.

I was well aware of the power of silence, so I merely waited her out. After a long pause, she lifted her head. "I told him if he didn't go away, I'd make sure he regretted it if it was the last thing I ever did."

Given where we were, it certainly looked like Marti Alexander had kept her word.

FOUR

MARTI ALEXANDER PROCLAIMED her innocence for a bit longer, and then we walked over to the precinct and questioned her further. Finally, we took her statement and her cell phone and let her go. When she left, I felt tired. I looked at my watch. It wasn't lunch time, but I felt like I'd been put through the wringer.

"I need a coffee."

Harley stretched. "I need something stronger than coffee."

I smiled. "Let's go."

He looked shocked. "I was just joking."

"Let's grab a good coffee from the St. Joseph Chocolate Factory." I grabbed my jacket and headed outside.

We drove the short distance to the café, which was always crowded. However, we lucked out and found seats near the back just as our coffees were ready.

We sat and drank in silence for a few seconds. I knew Harley had something on his mind by the way he kept staring at me when he thought I wasn't looking. Finally, I put my cup down and stared. "What?"

For a moment, he looked as though he intended to deny he had a question. "Did you believe her story?"

I sipped my coffee and sorted through my thoughts. Eventually, I shrugged. "I don't know."

"RJ, I don't think she did it."

I grinned and took another sip of my coffee.

"What's so funny? I'm serious."

"I know you're serious. That's what makes it funny."

He stared at me for a few seconds but eventually chuckled and sat back in his seat. "Okay, I'll admit it. I like her, but that doesn't change the facts. Her ex-husband sounds like a real jerk."

"Being a jerk isn't a crime worthy of death. If it were, there wouldn't be very many people left alive."

"He was a violent alcoholic with a gambling problem. For all we know, there might have been at least a dozen people with a reason to kill him."

We had learned about his gambling and alcohol addiction, along with several other bad habits, when Marti gave her statement. "You've been a cop long enough to know most people are killed by their nearest and dearest."

"But—"

I held up a hand. "He was unfaithful. He dumped her for another woman. He came to the house looking for his wife. He was drunk." I ticked off each thing as I mentioned it. "She owned a gun—"

"She left the gun at their old house when she moved out, and we don't even know if that was the same gun that killed him."

"We've only got her word for it that she left the gun." I could see Harley about to react, so I stopped him. "Everything I said is a good reason why she should be number one on our list of suspects. But, if we needed more, she doesn't have an alibi."

"That proves she's innocent."

"Maybe you didn't hear me. She does *not* have an alibi."

"If she had killed him, she would have made certain she had an alibi. Most innocent people don't have alibis."

He was grasping at straws now, but I let him continue.

"Besides, we don't know that she doesn't have an alibi. The new wife might be able to alibi her, and we haven't checked out whether anyone saw her leave the house."

I stared at Harley for a few moments and tried not to laugh. I wasn't successful.

"Why are you laughing?"

"You have it bad." I smiled. "I can't wait to tell Mama B."

We finished our coffees and went in search of Mrs. Harrison.

According to Marti, after Carolyn Harrison had learned about her husband's death, she moved out of Marti's home and returned to her own. So, that's where we headed.

Jake and Carolyn Harrison lived in the suburbs east of St. Joseph, Indiana. This was an area that was mostly farmland when I was a kid. Now, developers had bought most of the land and turned it into a gigantic labyrinth of subdivisions. Rangerton was basically one cookie-cutter subdivision after another. There were subdivisions for every taste and price range. Rangerton wasn't as big as St. Joseph, but it catered to new families and empty-nesters. Families could purchase their American Dream in Rangerton regardless of their financial situation. A house with or without the picket fence was available in a variety of sizes. Small villas and town-homes to luxurious estates on acres of land were available for a price. White flight from the city of St. Joseph meant the area wasn't known for ethnic diversity. However, one thing the area was known for was its school system. Unlike St. Joseph schools that struggled to pay teachers and provide technology for the students, Rangerton had one of the area's largest high schools, with everything from full media and production capability to fully stocked and funded art and theatre departments. Parents flocked there in droves, leaving the city of St. Joseph to escape the dwindling tax base, archaic buildings and infrastructure that needed massive renovations and teacher shortages.

Carolyn and Jake Harrison lived in one of the more prestigious subdivisions. A few months ago, Paris and I had attended a big tour known as the "Builder's Showcase." Builders opened the doors of homes they'd built on spec. The Builder's Showcase was free and provided potential buyers an opportunity to see the quality and craftsmanship of builders across the area. The local building association provided a free map, and for two weekends, anyone was welcome to drive around, find the homes and walk through. As an added bonus, most of the homes were furnished by area decorators to help potential buyers imagine themselves in these mini mansions. Neither Paris nor I was interested in purchasing, even if we could have afforded them. However, Paris was renovating an old Georgian home in the historic district, and the Builder's Showcase helped with design ideas, at least that's what she said. We spent a lot of time looking at window treatments.

Walnut Cove was a gated subdivision in Rangerton, but we showed the guard our shields to gain entry.
I pulled up to a semi-circular driveway in front of a
massive white brick French Country style home that
was brand new but made to look old. The house had
large timber beams, copper gutters and a slate roof that
must have cost more than Harley and I made in a year.
I pulled in behind a black 1969 Chevy Camaro Z28/SS
coupe with two broad white stripes that ran down the
hood and across the trunk. It was a muscle car and in
great shape. I loved cars and was surprised to see this
vintage model here. I hadn't taken Jake as a car enthu-
siast, but then I didn't really know him.

The house was impressive. Harley was born into a
wealthy family, but even he whistled when we got out of
the car. "This place looks massive. A gated subdivision
with twenty-four-hour security on a golf course over-
looking a man-made lake, now that's the life."

"Probably. But Jake Harrison is still dead." I went
up to the front door and rang the bell.

Within a few moments, an older woman with white
hair answered the door. "May I help you?" She looked
confused. I'm guessing she was accustomed to security
notifying her when visitors arrived.

We flashed our shields.

She frowned but stepped aside so we could enter.

"Is Mrs. Carolyn Harrison home?" I asked.

"She's resting. It's been a very traumatic few days,
but if you two will follow me into the living room, I'll
let her know you're here."

She led the way into an immaculately decorated
room with large overstuffed furniture that looked as

though someone had walked into a showroom and simply bought the floor models. This wasn't furniture that had been accumulated over time and passed down from one generation to the next. It was brand new furniture that had been purposely distressed and aged.

Our guide directed us to sit and then turned and headed out of the room.

Harley stared at the massive ceiling with wood beams and large windows and whistled again. "How do you think they change those lightbulbs?" He stared at a massive chandelier that hung from the ceiling.

"We hired someone to do it."

We turned and saw a woman who was stunningly beautiful. She was model thin with ripped jeans and a loose sweater that fell off the shoulder to reveal she couldn't possibly be wearing anything underneath. She wore a brightly colored scarf around her neck that complemented her thick blond hair, large blue eyes and pouty red lips. She was attractive, but overly made up with perfectly arched brows and meticulous makeup. She reminded me of the women in those *Housewives of* shows. I didn't like her, but that was probably because I didn't like women Mama B referred to as *homewreckers*. If Marti's story were to be believed, Carolyn had an adulterous affair with Jake Harrison for several years before she'd discovered the two together. However, adultery was no longer a crime in Indiana, not anymore anyway, and I knew it took two to tangle. If Marti and Percy were to be believed, Jake Harrison had "tangled" with a lot of women while he was married, so Carolyn was probably no more to blame than he was.

She smiled and flopped down onto the sofa. "Please sit down."

Harley and I sat. "I'm Detective RJ Franklin from the St. Joseph Police Department, and this is Officer Harley Wickfield."

She nodded at each of us.

"You have a lovely home, Mrs. Harrison, and that's a lovely scarf."

She smiled and grabbed the end. "It's just an old scarf I picked up somewhere." She was barefoot and tucked her legs under her on the sofa. "I take it this is about my husband's death. How can I help you?"

I was grateful she wasn't emotional. That would definitely make things a lot easier, but I couldn't help wondering why she wasn't. "You have our condolences on the death of your husband, but we do need to ask you a few questions—"

"If you're up to it of course," Harley said. He smiled broadly and turned up his Southern charm meter a bit so his accent was more pronounced.

She smiled. "Of course. Please, ask me anything."

Harley took out a notepad and pen.

"Mrs. Harrison, when was the last time you saw your husband alive?" I asked.

She took a few seconds to think. "You must know that my husband and I were…estranged. He was…tortured."

"What do you mean?"

She removed her scarf and pulled her hair back away from her face, exposing a dark greenish bruise.

I had a sister and spent a lot of my formative years around women, so I had developed a hatred for men who hit women. However, as a cop, I needed to remain unbiased. I took a few deep breaths and forced myself not to turn away. "Harley, you should take some pictures. That is if it's okay with you, Mrs. Harrison."

She nodded.

Harley pulled out his cell phone and snapped a few pictures. When he finished, he sat down. "Thank you."

"Of course, although I don't see how pictures of me will help you find a killer."

"We never know what may be helpful," I said. "Did you file a police report about the domestic violence?"

She chuckled. "No, I didn't want to make things worse. I just grabbed my coat and left."

"Where'd you go?"

"I know this is going to sound strange, but I went to my husband's ex-wife's house."

"Are you friends with your husband's ex-wife?" I already knew the answer, but I stared at her closely to gage her response.

"Actually, we weren't friends. You see, she resented me. She blamed me for ending her marriage."

"Did you?" I asked.

She paused. "I can see how you might think that, but it's not true. Their marriage was over long before I came into the picture." She tossed her head back. "Besides, if she wasn't able to keep her husband satisfied, well…"

For a brief moment, a look of triumph flashed across her face, and I thought I was getting my first glimpse into her true nature. However, she quickly replaced her mask and the expression disappeared.

"How long were you having an affair with Mr. Harrison while he was married?" Harley said, looking up from his notes. I noted a bright patch of red rise from her neck.

She huffed. "Really, I don't see what any of this has to do with my husband's death."

"We need to understand everyone who might have had a reason to want your husband dead," Harley said. *"Hell, hath no fury like a woman scorned."*

Carolyn Harrison scooted up taller in her seat and smiled. "Well, I know Marti was furious when she first found out about us."

"Wouldn't that be rather normal?" I asked.

"I would have expected her to maintain a certain amount of dignity." She rolled her eyes. "A woman has her pride, after all. But that was such a long time ago."

"How long?"

She paused. "Six months."

"So, you and Jake Harrison had been married for six months?"

"Just about, but we were together for at least a year altogether."

Harley looked up innocently. "Yet, when you fled your husband's abuse, you turned to his ex-wife, who you said was furious about the adultery?"

Carolyn's eyes narrowed, but she followed it up with a smile. "I know it seems odd, but I needed to find some place safe, some place where he couldn't find me. I grabbed my keys and ran out of the house, and I didn't have any place in mind. I mean, he would expect me to go to a hotel, but Marti's house was the last place he'd come looking for me."

"And Marti just opened her home to you?" I asked.

"She took a bit of convincing, but I was desperate. When she saw the bruises, she couldn't refuse."

"How long were you there?"

She thought. "I went there on Tuesday night, and I stayed until Sunday."

"You were with Marti Alexander Saturday night?" Harley asked.

She nodded. "Yep, we were together all night."

Here was a woman who was corroborating Marti's alibi. My head wanted to be grateful. I liked Marti Alexander. My girlfriend liked Marti, and now it looked like my partner liked her too. However, there were alarms ringing inside my head that were waving flags and screaming, *Danger, Danger, Will Robinson*. I exchanged a glance with Harley and then turned back to Carolyn Harrison. "May I use your bathroom?"

She gave me directions and then rose, but I assured her I could find it on my own, and Harley asked another question to keep her focused while I wandered through the house.

Cops are inherently nosy. I found the half bath and quickly looked around, but there wasn't much to see. The room was near the kitchen, and I glanced around there too.

The kitchen was massive. My entire townhouse would fit in this one room. There were a lot of French country kitchen cabinets, glazed to look aged and featuring distressed markings. The kitchen stove was massive and had at least eight burners and the red knobs Paris had taught me were the envy of home cooks. The counters were marble and looked as though they'd never been used. Although, given the fact there was a maid wandering around somewhere, I'm sure Carolyn was well fed. I noted two plates and two cups on the counter. I could tell Carolyn Harrison wasn't born into wealth. Despite her haughty attitude, her grammar and manners indicated she was a transplant into this world.

The maid wandered into the kitchen with a vase of flowers. She looked at me. "Can I help you?"

"No thank you. I was coming back from the bathroom. I must have taken a wrong term." I smiled. "This house is massive."

I could tell that she didn't believe me. She placed the flowers on the counter. "Follow me." She walked hard and didn't bother to turn and see that I was following her. When we got to the living room, she stopped and extended her arm.

I smiled at her. "Thank you."

She turned and went back the way we'd just come without another word.

We spent a few more minutes asking questions, but Carolyn Harrison wasn't giving up anything. Of course, she didn't really have to give up much. She had an alibi that covered both her and Marti. I knew I should be thankful. I could take it and run, but something inside wouldn't let me. "Mrs. Harrison, is there anyone who wanted to hurt your husband?"

She gave me a wide-eyed stare as though we hadn't just spent the last forty-five minutes talking about who had murdered her husband. "Not really, everyone loved Jake."

Obviously, *everyone* hadn't loved Jake or he wouldn't be lying on a slab in the morgue.

"Thank you for your time." I turned toward the door.

"Wait." She grabbed the long scarf that I'd admired

earlier and came very close and wrapped it around my neck. "Why don't you take this and give it to your wife."

"Thank you, but I'm not married." I started to remove the scarf that had a strong aroma of her perfume, but she halted me.

"That's okay." She smiled. "Maybe you'll find someone you can pass it along to."

Outside, Harley whispered, "I can't believe she was flirting with you while we were there talking to her about her husband."

She's probably one of those women who can't help herself. She flirts with all men. I took off the scarf and shoved it in my pocket.

We left, and I noticed the Camaro was gone when we went outside, but years as a cop had perfected my skill at remembering license plate numbers. When we got back to the precinct, I took Carolyn Harrison's scarf and shoved it into my desk drawer, sat down and ran the plates from the muscle car.

"What's with that look?" Harley said. He walked around my desk to stare over my shoulder at the computer screen. "Bruce Leonard? Why does that name sound familiar?"

"Because he used to be a cop. That is before he was investigated by Internal Affairs and then made a timely exit from the force."

"He hardly seems like Carolyn Harrison's type, does he? Why do you think he was there?"

"Inquiring minds want to know."

CHIEF MIKE BARINSKI wasn't as curious as I was. In fact, when Harley and I were called into his office to provide an update, he would have had to work hard to care less about why a former cop was at the home of the widow Harrison. Chief Mike was a large man, built like a middle linebacker. However, he was a highly dedicated cop and knew how to inspire his officers.

"There's no law against visiting someone's house. The victim, Jake Harrison, was a member of a prominent St. Joseph family, one of *the* most prominent families." He paced like a caged tiger in his tiny office.

"Not a crime," I said, "but isn't it suspicious that Carolyn Harrison didn't introduce him and that he didn't come out to meet us?"

"Jake Harrison was a broker in his family's brokerage house. Maybe he went to find out about his investments? Maybe he's a long-time family friend? Maybe he's shagging the housekeeper?" Chief Mike paced faster. "Whatever his reason for being there, it's not a crime."

He was right. Visiting Carolyn Harrison wasn't a crime, but it definitely caused my radar to flash. I was engrossed in my own thoughts and didn't realize the chief was waiting for a response. "Sorry, what did you say?"

"What about the ex-wife?"

"She didn't do it," Harley said a bit too eagerly.

Chief Mike was pacing and didn't notice. "Yeah, that's what they all say."

"Marti Alexander is one of us." Harley hadn't noticed the look I gave. "Well, almost. She—"

"We're investigating everyone," I said, glaring at Harley. This time he caught the message and sat back in his chair.

Chief Mike was distracted. "Well, this is another hot

one." He stopped pacing and turned to face us. "You two seem to have gotten quite a few hot cases lately."

"What's so hot about this one?" I had a feeling but wanted confirmation.

"Money. Jake Harrison's family has a lot of it, and they don't mind throwing it around for political contributions." He flopped down in his chair. "I've been waiting for Mayor Longbow to call and ask for an update, but—"

The phone on his desk rang. He rolled his eyes and sighed. "That's him now." He glanced up at us. "Get this murder wrapped up and fast." He answered the phone with one hand and shooed us out of his office with the other.

Back at our desks, I could tell by the steel in his back and the thunder in each footstep that Harley was angry. Inside the station was no place to release that pent-up anger. "Come on." I walked past my partner, not waiting for his reply.

Outside, I headed for Adamo's Bakery, expertly located across the parking lot from the station. I didn't stop until I was inside and seated at one of the small bistro tables. Harley flung himself down in the seat, but I could tell the walk over had quelled some of his fury. By the time he was seated across from me, his anger was a gentle boil rather than a raging volcano.

I recognized our waiter as one of the owner's ten children, a dark-haired, dark-eyed young man named Angelo. We ordered two coffees, and he hurried away to bring them to us.

Harley's chest heaved, and I put up a hand to stop him from speaking. "Listen, you're going to need to calm down. Chief Mike is just doing his job." He opened his mouth to speak but stopped when Angelo came with our coffees. As soon as Angelo left, I intercepted the conversation again. "I need you to listen to me."

He released a heavy sigh and sat back, arms folded across his chest.

"You and I both know ninety-nine percent of the time, murders are committed by a family member or loved one. If you didn't know Marti and didn't have a crush on her, you would have suggested investigating her too."

He lowered his arms from his chest and averted his gaze.

"Jake dumped her for another woman," I said. "That is a strong motive. As policemen, it's our job to investigate everyone. We wouldn't be doing our jobs if we didn't investigate her, if for no other reason than to eliminate her as a suspect."

Harley dropped his head and relaxed his shoulders. "You're right."

"Chief Mike doesn't have anything against Marti. For *him*, it's not personal."

Harley picked up on the emphasis and the corner of his mouth twitched. "It's not *personal* for me either. She barely knows I exist, especially since I gave her a ticket."

I chuckled. "Yeah, that's not the best way to endear yourself."

We sipped our coffees in silence for a few moments.

The wheels inside Harley's brain were clearly turning. After a few seconds, he said, "RJ, you don't believe she did it, do you?"

I thought for a few moments. "Let's just say I'm keeping an open mind."

He didn't like the answer, but he knew me well enough to realize it was the only one he was going to get.

We finished our coffee and were about to leave when my phone rang. I looked at the number and realized it was Paris. Before I could get the greeting out, she started.

"RJ, I need a favor. I'm at my shop, and I should be home letting Maya out and getting her ready to go to obedience class. Any chance you can swing by the house?"

I glanced at my watch, but I knew I was going to agree. "Of course."

She gasped. "Oh, wait. Never mind. You have to teach tonight. I totally, forgot—"

"It's okay. I don't have class tonight. We're on fall break."

"That's such a relief."

"Why don't I take her to Marti's for training and you can meet us there?"

She agreed.

I got up and left the money for two coffees on the table. "Come on, let's go help you get some face time with a dog trainer."

I drove to Paris's house, a large Georgian home in St. Joe's historic district, once the preferred area for St. Joe's elite with cobblestone streets, quaint carriage houses in back and views of the St. Joseph River. Paris's house, like all of the homes on her block, sat atop a hill with an expansive front lawn. Mama B said you can tell how wealthy people were by how far their homes were from the street. She was probably right in most cases, but St. Joe's historic district had slipped from the ranks over the years as the cost of upkeep and maintenance, not to mention taxes, failed to keep up with the economy and trends of convenience. Fewer people were interested in spending tens of thousands to renovate a 200-year-old house when you could build a bigger, modern, technology-laden home for less money in the suburbs. Meanwhile, the traffic, businesses and bustle of the city encroached more and more into what had once been an exclusive area but was now a passthrough on the way to gated subdivisions and man-made lakes like the ones in Jake Harrison's subdivision.

Paris's house had been abandoned for years and had fallen into so much disrepair, she'd managed to buy the house from the city for one dollar. She'd spent a small fortune making it into a home, and she wasn't finished.

Harley and I got out, and I used the key she'd given me to enter. I immediately went to the control panel to disarm the alarm system I'd insisted she get installed after she'd had a break-in. As a cop, I knew the alarm wouldn't deter a burglar intent on entering, but it might give her time to get out and would alert the police. Most importantly, it made her feel safe.

We heard Maya barking from the moment we entered, and I hurried to release her from her crate and get her outside to take care of business before she had an accident.

Maya barely made it outside before she was forced to stop, squat and answer the call of nature. She took a few sideways glances in Harley's direction while taking care of business. When she was done, she gave him a good sniff. She must have deemed him acceptable because her tail wagged and she allowed him to pet her.

"Come on, Maya." I gently pulled her leash and guided her back inside for the treat she knew would be her reward for going potty outside.

Once inside, I went to the ceramic jar Paris kept near the door. Maya rose on all four legs, paws on my waist. "Off."

She made a few circles, sat down and got up, full of energy. However, she eventually remembered the drill and forced her butt onto the floor, her tail wagging. She shook from the strain of not moving when there was a biscuit waiting.

I didn't torture her long. "Good girl." I handed her the dog biscuit.

She nearly took off two of my fingers in her eagerness, but I had learned over the weeks to watch for the signs and avoided a mishap.

"Geez!" Harley said. "She's quick. What's in those things, crack?"

"Beats me." I walked to the refrigerator and grabbed a couple of packs of string cheese and the duffle bag from the counter.

Harley was on his knees getting a tongue bath from the overzealous poodle who had been crated most of the day with only the sound of jazz playing from the surround-sound speakers Paris had installed.

I turned toward the circular device on the marble countertop. "Alexa, turn off the music." I looked down at Harley. "You two ready or do you need a room?"

He stood up and gave Maya a quick pat. "I'm surprised Paris has an Amazon Echo. She doesn't seem like the type for it."

The Amazon Echo was a smart, voice-controlled device that allowed you to control various devices, ask questions, search the web and control your other smart devices. "Are you saying Paris isn't technologically savvy?"

Harley's ears turned red and a moment of panic crossed his face as he realized he'd just criticized my girlfriend. "Ah…no, I mean. Paris just seems more… old school and not into gadgets. Not that there's anything wrong with that. I mean—"

I took pity on him and grinned. "It's okay, I said the same thing when I found out she had one." I grabbed the long leash from a hook on the back wall. "It was a birthday gift from her brother."

Harley heaved a sigh of relief.

We trotted outside. I rearmed the alarm system, closed and locked the door. I opened the car's back door for Maya, and she leapt onto the backseat. Harley took his place in the passenger seat.

H.O.T. Dog Training was located in a small brick building with a tin roof on the northside of town. Once a brick ranch in a secluded area, it was now on a busy thoroughfare next to a string of fast food restaurants that had inched closer and closer to residential homes.

From the street, there was nothing to indicate the property was anything but a residential house. I turned onto the very long driveway that skirted the side of the house and went back toward a long aluminum-clad outbuilding. There were three other cars parked on a concrete pad. I pulled next to the fence and parked.

Maya paced on the backseat, eager to get out and play.

I exited the car and attached her leash before allowing her to jump down. Then, Harley and I walked toward the outbuilding and entered.

Inside, the building was basically a barn that had been converted into a training facility. The majority of the building was open, but a small area had been sectioned off and separated with a wall. I knew from experience there was a small office area and a half bathroom. In the main area, there were a few foldup chairs placed near the side of the room. The floor was concrete, but a large rubber mat covered the middle section. Attached to the unfinished walls were various types of equipment that Marti used for her other dog training classes.

Harley, Maya and I found a place near the wall. I had the advantage of having been here before with Paris, so I was somewhat familiar with the routine. Harley's gaze roamed the building until Marti came through the back door. She was hauling a plastic collapsible tunnel that squeezed together like an accordion, making it easier to carry. Nevertheless, Harley hurried over to relieve her of her burden.

Marti looked puzzled to see him for a moment but quickly declined his offer, and with one swing, she hoisted the tunnel onto a shelf in the corner like a farmer tossing hay bales for cattle.

Callie trotted alongside her owner. At Harley's approach, Callie had stopped to give him a good sniff, which included the hand he extended, his leg and his crotch. He remained perfectly motionless until the examination was over. Eventually, Callie must have deemed him acceptable, as she climbed up on her hind legs and proceeded to give his face a good wash.

Harley made a typical rookie mistake and laughed. That's when Callie decided the inside of his mouth needed cleaning as well as the outside. He tried to back up but tripped over a bubble in the rubber mat and tumbled onto his butt, which gave Callie better access. The large standard poodle climbed onto his chest and pinned him down with her two front paws, continuing her thorough cleaning of Harley's face and neck.

I was so engrossed in watching the spectacle in the middle of the floor, I hadn't noticed Paris's arrival until she whispered in my ear. "What's he doing?"

I chuckled. "Trying to make a good impression with Marti, I think."

Paris took the duffle bag I was carrying. "Looks like he's getting better acquainted with Callie." She hurried to the restroom to change.

After a few seconds, Harley reached into his pocket and pulled out a white handkerchief. He waved it in the air. "I surrender."

Everyone laughed.

The corners of Marti's mouth twitched. After a few seconds, she called Callie to her side. "Callie, heel."

Callie immediately ceased Harley's spit bath and moved to Marti's left side. She positioned her shoulder to her owner's leg, sat and looked into her owner's eyes. Her mouth was open, her tongue hanging out. If I didn't know better, I'd swear she was laughing.

Marti extended her hand and helped Harley to his feet.

Harley dusted off his pants and used his handkerchief

to wipe his face. From where I stood, I could see his neck and ears were bright red. However, he played it off well.

Harley glanced down at Callie. "You could at least buy me dinner first."

Everyone laughed.

"Mr. Wickfield, if you and Callie are done, we need to get started." Marti extended her arm toward the wall, and Harley hurried back to where Maya and I stood.

Marti nodded at me and then started giving instructions for the other people in the class.

Paris hadn't returned from changing out of her work clothes. As a hair stylist and owner of two salons, she was able to dress very casually. Her old salon, which was located *in the hood* and serviced a primarily African-American clientele, was closed on Mondays, like most beauty salons. However, her newest salon, *Un jour à Paris*, an upscale salon located in a renovated downtown warehouse, was open on Mondays. In fitting with the locale and clientele, she tended to dress in a more professional manner, which I knew she wouldn't have wanted covered in dog hair. Poodles were known for their hypoallergenic coats and didn't shed. However, there were more than poodles in the training class, and dog hair flew through the air and covered nearly every flat surface.

The first exercise was getting your dogs to come when called. Marti instructed the class to release the energetic puppies that were lunging to run and play from their leashes. Maya, a German shepherd, a curly haired dog Paris told me was a golden retriever and poodle mix called a golden doodle and a border collie all ran into the middle of the floor, and a fierce game of chase followed.

The dogs played under the careful supervision of Marti for approximately two minutes. After which, she pulled a whistle from her pocket and blew it. "Call your dogs."

"Maya, come," I shouted.

None of the dogs responded but continued their game of chase.

We had been instructed to call our dogs one time and only once. If the dogs didn't come, we were to go, attach the leashes and guide our dogs back.

Maya saw me coming and immediately headed in my direction. I hooked her leash and walked her back to the bleachers, where Paris and Harley waited for us.

"Maya did great," Marti yelled. "Don't forget to praise her."

"Good dog." I petted her and handed the reigns to Paris, who mouthed a *Thank you.*

I waved goodbye to Marti, who nodded and continued to help the other owners get their dogs. Harley and I left.

We got in the car, and I headed for the station. He was quiet for the first ten minutes of the trip. Eventually, he cleared his throat. "Okay, that was a total and complete disaster. I can't believe I made a complete fool of myself."

"Actually, you may have found the one thing that would help endear you to her."

"You have got to be joking. Falling on my butt is not going to make her like me."

"Seriously, Marti loves dogs. If Callie didn't like you, then your chances of getting to Marti were slim to none."

"Too bad I don't want to date her dog."

I chuckled. "I'm serious. Dogs are a good judge of character. If her dog didn't like you, then you wouldn't have stood a chance. However, her dog seems to love you."

"Seems to? She practically forced herself on me."

"That's a good sign."

"I feel so violated."

We laughed all the way back to the station.

FIVE

ON THE WAY HOME, I got a call from Mama B asking me to come by. I was tired, but it was unusual for her to call, and there was something in her voice that made me think there was more behind her request. "Is everything okay?"

"Of course. Sister Green asked me to bake something for the senior choir's bake sale."

My heart raced. After she and Paris had been held at gun point, I made sure both women knew a code word they could use to alert me that they were in danger. I waited to see if she would use it.

"I decided to make a caramel cake."

"Did you make a rutabaga pie?"

She chuckled. "No, I did not."

I released the breath I'd been holding. Of all the things that Mama B baked, rutabaga pie was not one of them, so we knew it was a safe bet that if she ever called and told me she'd made a rutabaga pie, I would be safe in calling in the SWAT team. "Please tell me you made two." I noticed there was a bit of pleading in my voice.

She laughed. "I made two." She knew I loved her caramel cake.

"I'll be there in ten minutes."

I was pretty sure I made the trip in five minutes. I pulled up to the house and had to force myself not to run.

Mama B wasn't sitting on the porch, but the front door was open. When I got to the door, I saw her in her recliner.

"Come on in."

I didn't realize she had company until I was inside. I kissed her cheek and turned to take my seat on the end of the sofa. That's when I saw Chris Green.

"Hi, RJ." Chris and I slapped hands and did a one-armed man hug.

"I didn't realize you were here." I stared at Chris up close and personal. He looked fine. His eyes were clear. There were no visible tattoos or anything else to indicate gang affiliation. Since his last encounter with the Skulls, he appeared to have been scared straight and was keeping his promise to stay out of trouble. He jiggled his leg nervously. Clearly something was bothering him.

"Why don't y'all go in the kitchen and help yourself to some cake." Mama B rocked. "And I have some ice cream in the icebox."

Chris and I followed the sweet smell of caramel into the kitchen. The Formica table with metal legs held two cake containers. One container was made of glass. It was Mama B's good china, and she only used it for special occasions. The church bake sale would be one of those occasions. The other container was a cheap plastic cake container.

I lifted the plastic lid. On a plastic plate sat a three-layer cake with light brown, caramel icing. I couldn't stop myself from taking a deep breath of the sweet smell.

I turned to Chris. "You get the ice cream out of the freezer, and I'll tackle this cake."

He walked the few feet to her refrigerator and came back to the table with a yellow tub of vanilla ice cream.

I took two plates from a cabinet and silverware from a nearby drawer. Then, I took the cake cutter she had left on the table and cut two large pieces of cake and placed them on the plates. We scooped out large helpings of ice cream and then sat down.

Neither one of us said anything for several moments while we enjoyed the warm cake and ice cream. After a few moments longer, I looked up at Chris. "Now, why don't you tell me what's bothering you."

Years on the police force had taught me to read body language, and Chris's body language was screaming he needed to talk but wasn't sure if he should. From his nervous leg jiggle to his finger tapping and darting eyes, everything he did spoke volumes.

He took a deep breath. "RJ, man, I don't know what to do. I don't want no trouble."

I held up my hand. "Just tell me what's bothering you."

"My guidance counselor told me I needed to look for a job that would help show what a well-rounded person I am." He rolled his eyes. "You know, for when it comes time to work on my college applications. He wanted me to get a job working with disabled kids or something that would look good on the application, but that's just not my thing. So, I got this part-time job working on computers at Maxwell Loan Services."

I felt my chest tighten. "Maxwell Loan Services? Don't you need to be eighteen to work there?"

Maxwell Loan Services was one of those payroll advance places that preyed on the poor by offering loans at outrageous interest rates. An abundant amount of such storefronts were located throughout the poorer neighborhoods, along with "buy here, pay here" car lots and stores that sold everything from frozen pizza to pregnancy tests for one dollar.

"You have to be eighteen to work the money window. I'm just doing some back-office work on his computers." He smiled. "Actually, I was just helping out my aunt Marcia. She owns her own cleaning business, Aunt Marcia's Commercial Cleaning. She and Uncle Leo have a lot of contracts to clean buildings around town. Uncle Leo fell off a ladder and broke his leg, and she was upset because they just got the contract to clean all the Maxwell Loan buildings, and with Uncle Leo out, things got behind. She didn't have enough workers and needed help fast. So, I said I'd help out."

"Okay, but that sounds like you were working for your aunt's business. How'd you end up working for Mike Maxwell?" I tried not to stress out, but when I realized I was gripping the handle of my fork a bit too tightly, I placed it on my empty plate.

"Right, so I was working for Aunt Marcia, but when I was there, Mr. Maxwell just happened to be at the office we were cleaning. He was working late and complaining because his computer was acting up." He worked to hide a smile. "That's when my aunt starts telling him how good I am with computers and how I'd fixed their computer recently. Mr. Maxwell must have been desperate because he said, *If you think you can figure it out, have at it.*" He shrugged. "So, I sat down and that's when I saw he just had a virus. I downloaded a virus protection program and cleaned his computers, and he was back up and running by the time Aunt Marcia finished cleaning." He sat up straighter and stuck out his chest. He was obviously proud of his ability. I knew he liked working on computers and planned to major in computer science in college.

"You fixed his computer and…?"

"He was so happy, he gave me two hundred dollars and offered me a job working on his computers, making sure the whole network was free of viruses and setting up some tougher security."

I nodded slowly. Mike Maxwell was well known to the police. He was suspected of being involved in drugs, prostitution and money laundering. He was an extremely wealthy man, and we felt his legitimate businesses were merely a front to cover for his illegal activities. However, we had yet to prove him guilty of anything. I didn't like the idea of Chris Green, or anyone else I cared about, working for Mike Maxwell, even on a consulting basis. "So, what happened? This story seems like good news, but obviously something's bothering you."

He hung his head for a moment and then took another deep breath. "The other night, when I was working on the computer system, it was late and I had to go to the bathroom. Mr. Maxwell was out in the main area and somebody came in to talk to him. I didn't want to disturb him, so I went outside to…you know…take a leak. Well, the building backs up to an alley, so I went around back so no one would see me, but I didn't realize where I was going was under a window by where Mr. Maxwell was discussing business."

"You overheard something?"

He nodded.

"Did anyone see you?"

He shook his head slowly.

"What did you hear?" I took out a small pad and a pen from my pocket.

He paused and then started to talk very slowly and softly. "I heard Mr. Maxwell and another man."

"Did you recognize the man?"

He shook his head. "I never saw him, but Mr. Maxwell called him Jake."

That shocked me, but I recovered quickly. There were probably thousands of men in St. Joe named Jake. The fact that I had a corpse with the same name was most likely a coincidence. If I believed in coincidences. "What day was this?"

"Friday night about ten."

"Kind of late to be working, isn't it?"

"Aunt Marcia drops me at the office when she starts her cleaning rounds. Mr. Maxwell has five offices. She can't start cleaning until the office is closed. So, at eight, she drops me at the main office and then goes to take care of the other four. I usually empty the trash cans, sweep and make sure the restroom is clean and then get busy with the computers. Aunt Marcia swings by to make sure the office is up to her standards. Then, she locks up and takes me home. Normally, Mr. Maxwell isn't there late."

"Did he know you were in the office?"

"Yeah, but he closed the door where I was when the guy... Jake came."

"So, if you were in the office, you wouldn't have been able to hear their conversation?"

"No, because Mr. Maxwell has another office at the other side of the building. The only reason I was able to hear them was because I was outside...well, you know."

Yeah, I knew. "What did you hear?"

Chris swallowed hard. "Mr. Maxwell was mad. He cussed a lot and told the other guy...Jake...he was tired of excuses. Either he paid the twenty thousand dollars he owed or Mr. Maxwell would have to make an example of him." Chris's hands were shaking and the jiggle in his leg, which had stopped for a few moments, returned. "RJ, I was scared. He sounded serious, and I could tell that Jake sounded scared."

"What did Jake say?"

"He begged Mr. Maxwell. He said he'd get the money, but he needed more time. His family found out he'd been taking money from the business and they cut off his access. He said his grandfather had set up a trust, but he needed his ex-wife's help to get to the money."

"Did he mention her name?"

Chris thought for a few moments. "It sounded like Marcy or something like that."

I took a moment to make sure my question sounded casual. "Could he have said Marti?"

Chris sat up and snapped his fingers. "That's it. Marti. He said he needed Marti's help to get to the money. He begged Mr. Maxwell to give him more time." He paused and dropped his head. "Mr. Maxwell said he'd already given Jake more time than he deserved because of his family connections, but his *patience had waned.*" He used air quotes. "He said Jake was more trouble than he was worth and he may get more pleasure from killing him than he would from the fifty thousand dollars." He shivered and shook his head. "RJ, he sounded so cold."

"What happened next?"

"I saw headlights pulling into the parking lot and figured that had to be my aunt coming to pick me up. So, I finished up and hurried back inside."

"Did anyone see you?"

"No, I'm pretty sure they didn't."

"And you didn't see Jake?"

"No. When Aunt Marcia came, I had my backpack and was ready to get out of there. Mr. Maxwell came out of the office and closed the door behind him, so we couldn't see who was in the office with him." He looked up at me. "He came over with a big smile on his face and slapped me on the back like nothing had happened. He was grinning like he hadn't just threatened to kill somebody."

"What did you do?" I held my breath, hoping I wouldn't hear anything that would make me concerned for Chris's safety.

"I just said thanks and went to the car."

I reached out to him. "Chris, this is really important. Do you think he suspected you may have overheard him?"

He shook his head. "Nah, I'm pretty sure he didn't."

I took a deep breath and released the grip I had on my pen. "That's good. So, that was Friday night. Have you been back?"

He shook his head. "I only go on Tuesday, Thursday and Saturday."

"Tomorrow is your next workday?"

He nodded.

"I'm going to need you to come down to the station and make a formal statement." He immediately started to shake his head, but I stopped the geyser I sensed was about to erupt inside him by saying, "You're going to have to trust me. We need to ask you more questions and get everything you remember down on paper—"

"If Big Momma finds out, she's going to flip her wig."

"We're going to have to tell her, but we'll tell her together."

"RJ, I don't know, man. I mean lots of people threaten to kill people. They don't mean it. Maybe he was just trying to scare this Jake. Maybe they're old friends or something. It might not have meant anything at all." He stood up and looked ready to run.

I stood too. "Chris, you're right. It might have been an idle threat…just words to scare someone who owed him money into coughing up the cash."

He nodded vigorously. "Yeah, I'm sure that was all it was."

"Or it could be a lot worse. I don't want to scare you, but Mike Maxwell is a very dangerous man, and a man named Jake Harrison was murdered Saturday night."

The color left his face. He swayed and would have collapsed if I hadn't helped him back to his seat.

"Put your head between your legs."

He complied. After a few moments, he lifted his head. "You okay?"

He nodded, but his hands were shaking and the leg jiggle had progressed to a gallop. I stood and went to the cabinet and got him a glass of water.

He had to use both hands to keep from sloshing the

water on the floor. After a few sips, he put the glass on the table. "I don't think I should say anything. I don't want to make a statement. I shouldn't have said anything at all. I should have kept my mouth shut. In fact, that's what I'm going to do. I'm going to keep my mouth shut. He doesn't know I heard anything. If I keep quiet, he'll never know that I heard him." He looked at me. "Unless you tell him."

"Chris, it's important that we get the truth. If Mike Maxwell killed someone, then we need to lock him up, and you can help us." I stared down at a terrified kid who I'd known since he was a baby. "However, if you don't want to make an official statement, I won't say anything."

The relief passed over him like waves on a beach. "Thank you, RJ. Yeah, that's what I want. I don't want to make a statement. I didn't see or hear anything."

The cop in me wanted to convince him to come forward and make an official statement. I had speeches memorized that I'd used on other witnesses about the importance of coming forward, of how it was their duty as citizens and how the police couldn't do their jobs if people refused to help us. However, in the eyes of that teenage boy, I saw pure fear and knew that I couldn't convince him to come forward in good conscience. Instead of being a cop, I decided to be a friend. I made sure he had my cell phone number in case of emergency. I suggested he finish his assignment with Mike Maxwell as quickly as possible and not simply walk away so he wouldn't raise suspicion. I also promised to make sure the local police kept the building under surveillance,

especially on Tuesday, Thursday and Saturday nights
while he was in the building.

By the time his hands stopped shaking and his leg
slowed back down to a jiggle, it was dark outside. We
went back into Mama B's living room. She was reclined
in her chair and wearing a house dress with a scarf tied
around her head, Aunt Jemima style, with pink foam
curlers sticking out of the top and underneath one side.
She was watching an old episode of Columbo.

"RJ, when you drive Chris home, take that caramel
cake to Sis Green so she won't have to walk down here
to get it."

I turned around and went back into the kitchen.

"You might as well take that other cake to work," she
yelled. "God knows I don't need that sugar."

I grabbed both cakes and returned to the living room.
I gave the lighter of the two to Chris to carry and bent
down and gave Mama B a kiss.

"Make sure you save a piece for Paris and—"

"I know. I know. Don't forget to bring back your
Tupperware."

She smiled as Chris and I left.

Sister Green's house wasn't far, so the drive didn't
take long. But I changed my mind at least thirty times
in less than five minutes. One second, I was determined
to persuade Chris to come forward, the next second, I
wanted him to be safe. As a cop, I knew there was no
way we could completely guarantee his safety. If anything went wrong, and Chris or his grandmother were
hurt, I would never be able to live with myself. I went
back and forth like a pendulum on a grandfather clock

until I pulled up at the house and Chris got out with one of the caramel cakes.

"Chris…"

He turned back toward me, although his eyes refused to meet mine. After a long pause, he eventually raised his eyes. The look made my decision for me.

"Tell your grandmother I asked about her."

He nodded. "Thanks, RJ."

His comment could have been for the ride or for asking after his grandmother. However, I knew with every fiber of my being that it was related to the fact that I hadn't pressured him to make a statement.

I waited until he got inside before pulling away. The conflict between the cop and the friend continued to wage war in my head. Ultimately, I knew I couldn't take the guilt of the death of another kid on my conscience. One was enough.

SIX

It wasn't a surprise when I didn't sleep more than two-hours. In fact, I half expected it. Sadly, I was learning to survive on less and less sleep. My doctor had given me pills to help, but I didn't like the way I felt afterward. I struggled to wake up, and my brain always felt cloudy. As a cop, I needed a clear head and sharp reflexes. I felt better with natural sleep, such as it was, and caffeine. Although, if I didn't sleep by the weekend, then I'd have to take the pills. Experience told me I couldn't go much longer than a week with the amount of sleep I've been getting.

At the office, I finished up my paperwork. Harley was needed on another assignment, so I was on my own. I spent some time looking up what we had on Mike Maxwell. He'd been charged with a number of crimes, but nothing that stuck. I scanned the computer for more but was just about to give up when my phone rang.

"RJ, do you have time to meet with me?" Judge E.L. Browning had retired from the bench and was now the dean of MACU's law school. He was also my mentor and friend.

I looked at the time. "Absolutely. You name the time and the place."

As the dean of the law school, Judge Browning was a busy man, so I wasn't surprised when he suggested we have lunch at one of the restaurants on campus.

I grabbed my jacket and headed out. Just as I was leaving, I ran into Detective Martinez.

"RJ, I was just on my way to see you."

"I was just heading out. Is it important?"

He handed me a report. "Just some preliminary findings on the body we pulled out of the river."

"Thanks." I took the file and glanced through it.

Detective Martinez was about five-eight with a medium frame. He was in his mid-twenties but looked older because of his shaved head, mustache and goatee. He was solid and ambitious.

"Walk with me."

Detective Martinez kept pace as we walked down the corridor.

"Obviously, there's something unusual here," I said. "Bottom line it for me."

He cleared his throat. "The shoeprints found at the scene match those of the contractor, Marti Alexander, who claimed to find the body."

"Well, considering she was there doing search and rescue, it would be natural to find her shoeprints on the scene."

"Yes, but she also *claimed* to have gotten a message on her cell telling her to go to the scene, but the St. Joseph Police Department didn't send that message."

This was information I already knew, so I was wondering where Detective Martinez was going. "Anyone could have sent that message. Were you able to trace it?"

"Unfortunately, not. It was probably sent from a burner phone." He smiled. "But I did find out that her phone pinged a cell tower near the crime scene early Saturday morning. So, she was there."

I stopped. "You're telling me Marti Alexander's cell phone pinged a cell tower near the place at the river where her ex-husband's body was found?"

He nodded. "I thought you'd want to know."

Well, that's just great. We'd made it to the door. "Thanks, Detective."

I thought about that cell phone all the way to MACU's campus. I parked outside of the MACU Inn.

Judge Browning was already seated at his favorite table near the window of the wood-paneled room when I arrived. He was engrossed watching a pair of squirrels playing outside the window and didn't notice when I approached the table.

"Good to see you, Judge. If you invited me here to fire me, can you at least wait until after I've eaten?"

Judge Browning chuckled. "Sorry, no such luck. Your class is so popular, I keep getting rave reviews from your students asking if they can retake the class."

I groaned and sat down opposite the judge.

When Judge Browning retired from the bench to take the position of dean of MACU's law school, he convinced me to teach an adjunct class for first-year law students about the practical side of the law: "Police, Law and Society." At first, I was reluctant and gave every possible objection I could think of. E.L. didn't listen and convinced me to give it a try and commit to one class for one single semester. I was terrified, but talking about police work came easy to me, and the students loved to hear about my real cases. In fact, I was surprised to learn that I was actually enjoying the class and my students a lot more than I ever dreamed I would.

"So, if I'm not fired, why did you invite me? Parental complaint?"

He shook his head. "No complaints. In fact, I was hoping I could convince you to take on another class next semester."

That was a shock. I was momentarily struck dumb.

Thankfully, the waiter arrived, and I was able to gather my thoughts while I perused the menu. Orders placed, I returned to the subject at hand.

"You're joking, right? I can't possibly take on another class. I'm a full-time policeman."

E.L. leaned across the table and gazed into my eyes. "You're looking tired, and I thought maybe you might want a bit of a break, especially after the accident."

I could feel the heat rise up my neck and took a drink of water to give myself a moment.

The waiter returned with our salads and bought me a little more time. However, he wasn't there nearly long enough for me to think how to respond. E.L., like most of my family, friends and the St. Joe Police Department, were all aware that I had been involved in a car accident a few months back. The accident was caused by a teen-aged girl who was texting and driving. She rear-ended me, and I hit another car. The accident was not my fault. However, the fact that I wasn't responsible didn't stop the guilt. I blamed myself for not swerving enough to avoid hitting the car in front of me. I blamed myself for not being able to save the toddler who died because the CPR I performed on her hadn't worked. I lived with the sight of her crushed body every time I closed my eyes and every time I woke up in a cold sweat in the middle of the night. I knew it was because I hadn't been quick enough, good enough or spiritual enough to save her. My reflexes, my CPR, my prayers all failed.

"RJ, I don't mean to pry, but over the past few months, we've gotten to be close. You're a good cop, and you're not to blame for that accident, but I know nothing I say or do is going to change your mind. Only you can do that. However, what I can do is offer you an opportunity to take a break. Step away from the police work for a bit. You mentioned that Chief Barinski offered you a chance to stay on as a consultant."

Judge Browning was on the short list of people with whom I'd shared that information, but he'd never tried to sway me in either direction before today.

I gave him a hard look. "Why do I think you've been talking to my godmother?"

He held up both hands. "Guilty." He chuckled but quickly got serious again. "Seriously, RJ, Miss Ella is concerned about your wellbeing. She loves you and… she means well."

"I know." I paused to collect my thoughts. "I can't say I haven't been thinking about it, but I've wanted to be a cop my entire life. I love what I do."

"Sounds like Chief Mike is giving you the opportunity to continue to be a cop, at least in some capacity." He picked up his fork and started to eat. "But I don't want to pressure you. I promised Miss Ella that I'd talk to you, and I have. However, I am selfishly hoping that you'll agree to take me up on my offer to teach more. Your students won't stop raving about you, and their friends who took the class earlier are lobbying to retake the class. Frankly, I just want to get them off my back."

I laughed.

We ate in peace, and Judge Browning made no further references to taking on additional classes. Our conversation centered around football and MACU's undefeated season. We contemplated which bowl game they would be invited to. When the waiter brought the dessert tray, we both opted for their chocolate molten lava cake and ate the first few bites in wonderous silence. The aroma of chocolate and vanilla beans from the ice cream wafted up to my nose with each bite.

When we were stuffed and relaxed, Judge Browning asked if I was working on the Harrison case.

I wasn't surprised that Judge Browning kept abreast of current murders, even though he wasn't on the bench anymore.

I nodded and quickly filled him in on the basics. I took the opportunity to mention I suspected Jake Harrison may have owed money to Mike Maxwell.

He frowned and shook his head. "I knew Jake had a gambling and a serious drinking problem, but I had no idea it progressed to the point where he needed to borrow money from a loan shark like Mike Maxwell."

"How did you know? Are you friends of the Harrisons?"

"I wouldn't exactly call us friends. We're more like friendly acquaintances. I sit on some of the same boards

as The General, and over the years, we've come to respect each other."

"The General?"

He chuckled. "Jake's grandfather. Apparently, his
mother had high aspirations. George Washington Wil-
liam Henry Harrison."

I whistled. "That's a mouthful. His mother couldn't
just name him after one United States President, she
named him after two?"

"If the power of a name had anything to do with it,
he would have been president. However, The General
had higher hopes than the office of president. He set out
to build himself an empire."

"Rich?"

"Rich doesn't even scrape the surface. When the gov-
ernment of small countries need money, they call The
General."

"Funny, I've never really heard about him."

He smirked. "That, my friend, is by design. The General is a very private man. He's practically a recluse,
but there are a few things that he is passionate about."

"So, if The General is so rich, then why was Jake
borrowing money from a loan shark? Why not just
borrow a wheelbarrow full of money from his grandfather?"

He thought for a moment. "The General started out
with nothing. He built a financial empire over time. He
worked hard, sacrificed and took risks. He believed anyone who didn't work twenty-four-seven to build their
wealth was just plain lazy."

"Even his own grandson?"

"Especially his grandson."

"Where's the father?"

Judge Browning smiled. "Richard followed in his father's footsteps and built an empire of a different kind."

Something in the judge's face made me probe. "Richard?"

Judge Browning's eyes twinkled, and he struggled to keep a straight face. "Richard Stonewall Humphrey Harrison." He paused and gave me a glance. "But you may know him by his stage name."

"Stage name? Is he some kind of actor?"

His lips twitched. "Some would call him an actor."

My brain drew a blank. "I'm going to need a little more to go on."

"When he was small, we used to call him Dicky… when he decided to make…ah…films, he used his nickname and shortened his middle names."

That name rang a bell. "Dicky…where do I know that name from?" I stared at the Judge, and that's when it came to me. "No way."

He nodded.

"Dick Stone…the…adult film star?"

Judge Browning laughed. "That's the one. I understand he performs using several variations on his names."

We both laughed.

"I'll bet The General wasn't pleased with that career choice."

The judge shook his head.

"This financial wizard's son is…" I leaned forward and whispered, "A porn star?"

Judge Browning nodded. "Apparently, he made a ton of money making—" he made air quotes "—art films overseas."

"Wow. I don't want to judge, but based on what you've told me about The General, I can't imagine that sat too well with him."

"He was furious. It was probably one of the first times when he wasn't able to bend the world to his command. But he sure tried. At first, he bought out every company that tried to produce one of the films, but that didn't stop Dicky. He just bought camera equipment and filmed himself. Initially, he posted them online and basically invented the entire online pornographic industry. Made a fortune."

"I guess The General couldn't buy the entire Internet. So, Jake Harrison's father's a porn star, and his grandfather's a financial genius. What about his mother?"

"Died in childbirth. Jake was raised by a succession of nannies and private boarding schools from one coast to the other."

I thought about that for a few moments. My parents didn't have a lot of money, but my sister and I always knew we were loved. I remember my dad working two jobs to keep food on the table. Yet he managed to make every basketball game, school play and, in my sister's case, debate match. My parents didn't have money, but they gave us the most valuable commodity they had: their time.

"Jake Harrison grew up to be a spoiled pampered brat," Judge Browning said. "He sailed through school on his grandfather's donations. When he graduated, The General set him up as president of one of his financial businesses, but Jake was ill-equipped to handle that type of responsibility. Frankly, I'm not surprised he wasn't successful, but I am surprised The General finally cut the purse strings."

"You think Jake turned to Mike Maxwell for the money he couldn't get from his father or his grandfather?"

"It's possible. The General was too controlling, and his father just didn't care enough to bother."

"What can you tell me about Mike Maxwell?"

He leaned back in his chair and thought for a few moments. "He started out in Chicago. He relocated to St. Joe over twenty years ago. As the story goes, he made an unsuccessful move on the turf of one of the local mob bosses, and the heat got too much."

"Ninety miles isn't far enough to escape the reach of a mob boss. If they wanted to kill him, they certainly could. He must have been connected."

"His connections were good enough to keep him alive, just not in Chicago. Anyway, he came here and started loaning money. When I was on the bench, he was arrested for everything from extortion to blackmail. The only problem was, we couldn't get any of it to stick. Witnesses had a habit of turning up dead."

I nearly choked but forced myself to remain calm.

"After a while, he settled into a groove. We suspected he was involved in some illegal activities, but nothing dangerous. I guess he found he could make more money through legitimate channels than he could on the underground. Maybe he's still at it, but if he is, he's gotten really good at staying under the radar."

Judge Browning and I chatted awhile longer, but he had another meeting, and I needed to get back to work. He had lunch put on his tab, and I promised to think seriously about teaching more classes.

Judge Browning declined a lift, and I sat in my car and watched him walk across the campus to his next meeting. I replayed the judge's voice over and over in my head. Eventually, I turned up the radio to drown it out. *Witnesses had a habit of turning up dead.*

SEVEN

WHEN I LEFT the parking lot, I couldn't help myself. I drove to the quick loan building where Chris had told me he met Mike Maxwell. A woman in her early twenties with purple hair and a nose ring told me Maxwell wasn't there. I was just about to leave when a large black Hummer pulled up to the curb. The music inside the vehicle was so loud, it shook the windows of the building. Even though the vehicle's windows were dark, I didn't need to look inside to know Mike Maxwell had arrived.

Maxwell was short and stocky. He wore a tight silk shirt unbuttoned to reveal dark chest hair and several gold necklaces, including a cross. I could tell just by looking that his shoes were expensive, handmade leather. He climbed down out of the Hummer and strutted inside. He walked like he owned the place, which technically he did, but there was an arrogance that made me want to knock him down a peg.

He flashed a toothy smile at purple hair, who giggled and blushed. He headed for his office but took a long glance in my direction.

I pulled back the side of my jacket, making my shield visible, and held his gaze. I wasn't sure what it was that connected cops and criminals, but there was something that enabled easy identification. For a brief second, his mask fell and I saw the contempt in his eyes, but he replaced it quickly and flashed his toothy white smile in my direction as he strutted toward me.

"It must be my lucky day." He extended his hand. "What can I do for you, Officer? You looking for a loan?" He glanced at purple hair and laughed.

I debated whether to shake his extended hand, but I wasn't ready to aggravate him yet. "No, I'm not here to borrow money, but I don't think I could afford your interest rates anyway."

He flinched and then glanced around the store.

There was a young woman with two small children in tow at the window with the purple-haired clerk and a slim young man wearing the greasy coveralls that identified him as a car mechanic waiting to approach the counter.

Maxwell flashed his smile again, but this time there was even less sincerity. "Then what brings you here?"

"Official business. Is there some place we could talk in private?"

Maxwell hesitated a half-second, but then he turned and walked to the counter. He pushed a button that released a half door, and he held it open while I followed. Once behind the counter, I followed him to a door on the right side of the room and waited while he unlocked the door. He entered and again held the door open for me.

The office was small, but extremely luxurious. There was a large desk that dominated the majority of the room and several guest chairs. The carpet was thick and plush.

Maxwell walked behind the desk and sat. He extended an arm, indicating I was to follow suit.

He leaned back in his chair and glanced at me. "Now, how can I help you, Officer...?"

It was a dance of dominance played by schoolboys on playgrounds across the country. The alpha walks through the doors first, sits first, talks first. We were on his turf, and he was in control. He was the top dog, and I was relegated to the role of underling. At least that was his intention.

It was an ancient dance, but I knew a few moves of my own. I countered his maneuver by continuing to stand. I was probably a foot taller than he was, and he would have to strain his neck to continue looking up at me. The longer I stood, the more uncomfortable he would be, both psychologically and physically.

"My name's Detective RJ Franklin, and I'm investigating the death of Jake Harrison."

Maxwell shifted in his chair. "Jake Harrison? I'm not sure I know..." He glanced upward as though trying to recall and then snapped his fingers. "Oh, yeah, tall, skinny, good teeth?" He looked at me as though expecting confirmation.

I stared back.

After a few seconds, he sighed. "Alright, you wouldn't be here if you didn't already know I knew him, so I'll admit it." He leaned back in his chair. "I have nothing to hide. Yes, I knew him. He came in wanting to borrow money. I loaned it to him. That's what I do."

"When was the last time you saw Jake Harrison?"

Again, he glanced up and to the right. "I don't know. He came in here a few days ago wanting an extension."

"Did you give it to him?"

"Yeah, I did. I'm overly generous that way." He

smiled. "I'm just an old softy." He chuckled. "Now he's dead, and I'll never see my money." He shrugged. "Such is life."

"How much did he owe you?"

"Twenty Gs."

I paused. "You loaned him twenty thousand dollars? I didn't know quick loan companies gave out that kind of money."

I could see a vein start to pulse on the side of his head, and the tops of his ears got red. He took a deep breath. "We don't. It was a personal loan."

"You loaned Jake Harrison twenty thousand dollars of your own money?"

"Yeah. He said he was in bad shape and really needed the money."

"You must have been good friends with him to have loaned him that much." He looked as though he was going to object, but I forestalled him by saying, "I mean, I can't imagine you'd loan that kind of money from your own pocket to a common stranger, right?"

He held my gaze for a few moments. "I didn't know him personally, but I know a good investment when I see one."

"Really?"

"Yeah, I'm in business to make money, so I learned to evaluate risks quickly." He leaned back again. "I wish you'd sit down, you're giving me a cramp in my neck." He waited.

I hesitated for a few seconds, but I'd made my point, so I sat.

"Jake Harrison was the grandson of the financial ge-nius folks call The General, estimated net worth in the

billions. His father made a wad of cash as a porn star."
He turned to me with a grin. "Ever seen any of his films?
He's got a really big—"

"I'm not interested in his father's films."

"Well, his father used his assets to make millions."

"What's any of that got to do with Jake Harrison?"

"I figured if junior didn't pay, then dad or granddad
would pony-up the money. Neither of them would want
to have word get around that their progeny welched on
his debts."

"Did it work?"

Maxwell lowered his gaze and stretched his neck.
"No. Apparently, junior had worn out his welcome with
granddad."

"What about his father?"

He hesitated and then reluctantly said, "His dad could
have cared less." He snorted. "That man has the foulest
mouth I've ever heard. He actually told me to go f—"

"Yeah, I get it."

He extended his hands in a pleading manner. "I
mean, what is this world coming to when parents take
that kind of attitude?"

I almost laughed at his frustration, but this was no
laughing manner. "Did you threaten him?"

He looked innocent. "I don't know who you've been
talking to, but I would never threaten another human
being."

"Did you kill Jake Harrison?"

The smile froze on his face. "I don't like where you're
going with this conversation, Detective."

We stared at each other like a couple of gunsling-
ers in a Western movie, waiting for the other person to

twitch. However, without guns, at least not visible, we merely stared. Eventually, Maxwell blinked. He threw his head back and laughed.

I continued to stare him down, even though it was a one-sided battle at this point. "Jake Harrison owed you a lot of money. He didn't pay. When he came here the night he died, did you laugh?"

As I expected, that halted his laughter. He narrowed his eyes and looked at me. "How did you know he came to see me?"

Our stare down was back on. "I know a lot of things about you."

He continued his narrow-eyed stare for a few moments but then plastered a fake grin on his face. "Detective, you should know better than to believe all the gossip you hear." He leaned back in his chair. "Accusations like that can get you sued for slander." He stared at me and reached for his cell phone. "I don't think I'm going to say anything else without my lawyer present."

"Got him on speed dial?"

He glared, cell in hand. "Am I under arrest?"

This time it was my turn to blink. "No." I paused. "Not yet anyway. However, I may have more questions for you."

He placed his cell phone on the desk. "I'm not going anywhere, Detective Franklin." He turned to his laptop and waved a hand in my direction. "I've got a lot of work to do. I'm sure you can see yourself out."

With a wave, I was dismissed.

I rose, turned and walked out of the room. If I were keeping score, despite that last point in Maxwell's favor,

I held the advantage and counted myself slightly ahead in our pissing match.

It took the entire drive back to the precinct before I was able to completely shake off the mental funk I felt after meeting with Mike Maxwell. The man was oily and left me feeling dirty and angry. He could have killed Jake Harrison. In fact, I hoped he had killed him. Locking him up for the murder would be the answer to a lot of problems. Not only would it take the pressure off Marti, it would take a dirty criminal off the streets. If I could tie Maxwell to Jake Harrison's murder, it would not only resolve this murder but keep Chris Green safe, and the streets of St. Joseph, Indiana, would be a lot safer too.

When I arrived at the precinct, Harley was waiting for me. Technically, Harley was only on loan to Special Crimes and often got called to work in other areas. I filled him in on what I'd learned from the judge, at least the items that pertained to the case. Then I filled him in on my visit to Mike Maxwell. I had one more stop to make, and this time, Harley was able to accompany me.

A short drive east of the precinct took us to an area of St. Joseph with large, older homes set back from the street with generous-sized lots, older trees and manicured lawns. The General's home was surprisingly smaller than I expected a financial genius to own, especially after seeing his grandson's mansion.

The house was a modest 1920s era home with partial brick exterior and partial aluminum. Don't get me wrong, it was a large home. If I had to guess, I'd say it was well over 3,000 sq. ft. However, this two-story traditional lacked the flash and over-the-top-opulence of his grandson's house. This was a charming home of understated elegance, which told me a lot about the General.

We rang the bell and were greeted by a friendly face, which I recognized immediately.

"Sister Young, I didn't know you worked here?"

Mattie Young was an older African-American woman. She attended the same church that I did and had cooked and cleaned for Pastor Hamilton for the past twenty years.

She smiled and pulled me close into a motherly bear hug. "RJ, it's so good to see you." She squeezed hard and then released me before merely nodding at Harley.

Harley and I had ransacked Reverend Hamilton's study while looking for evidence in a murder investigation several months ago. Thinking back on the incident, I struggled to keep from laughing, especially when I remember her threatening to take Harley over her knee. She had forgiven me due to a lifetime of shared memories, but she didn't have those same memories of Harley's life and was harboring some hurt feelings.

"We're here to see The General," I said. "Is he home?"

"Is it about Jake?" She shook her head. "You best come inside." She stepped back and allowed us to enter. Once inside, she closed the door. "I knew that poor boy would get up to no good."

"Did you know Jake Harrison?" I stared at Mattie Young, hoping I could get an unbiased opinion.

"Know him? I practically raised him after his poor mama died, what with his father off his head and The General, well…he didn't know nothin' 'bout raising no baby." She chuckled at the thought.

"I didn't even know you worked here. I thought you just worked at the church and for Reverend Hamilton."

"I've been doin' for The General for longer than you've been alive. I used to work here full-time, but after his wife died, well, he didn't need me every day, and I still needed to eat." She chuckled. "Although, I could probably stand to lose a few pounds."

A gruff voice called out, "Mattie, who was at the door? If it's another one of those blasted reporters, I'll have their head."

"You best come in and meet The General before he comes lookin' for you." She turned and led us down a hallway to a room at the back corner of the house. Even though the door was open, she stopped and knocked. "It's the police to see you, General." She stepped aside.

I heard a heavy sigh as Harley and I stepped past Mattie and entered the room, which had been fashioned into a study.

The room wasn't exceptionally large, but it had a bank of windows on one side that looked out over a garden, an expansive lawn and a pool. The house had been updated but not modernized, and the original radiators lined a section of the wall. As we walked across the room, I could tell by the squeaks, scratches and scuff marks that the floors were original.

There were two dominate features that stood out in that room. The first was a massive desk. It was oak with intricately carved details. The desk looked familiar, and after staring for several moments, I realized why. A love of woodwork and a lot of sleepless nights spent watching movies like *National Treasure* in the wee small hours of

the morning placed the desk as a replica of the Resolute
desk used by many United States presidents.

The other dominant feature in the room was the man
who sat behind the desk. Even seated, I could tell The
General was taller than average. He was burly, bald and
had thick bushy white eyebrows and a thick full mustache underneath a large bulbous nose on an otherwise
smooth-featured face.

"Well, don't just stand there. Sit."

Harley and I each sat in one of the leather guest
chairs that faced the large desk.

"My name is Detective—"

"I don't need introductions. You're Detective Robert
James Franklin from the St. Joseph Police Department's
Special Crimes division, although you prefer to be called
RJ." He stared at me for several seconds and then turned
his attention to Harley, giving him a smug look.

"You're Officer Harley Wickfield the fourth."

I tried not to let the irritation I felt come through my
voice. "You're very well informed."

"I didn't get where I am by waiting around for men
to come to me. I learned early on in life if you wanted
to succeed, you had to stay at least three steps ahead of
everyone else." He glanced from Harley to me and then
interlaced his fingers across his belly and leaned back.
"As you know, I've been very successful in my life."

The man was arrogant, and he rankled my ire.
"Maybe you could save us some time and tell us who
killed your grandson."

The General narrowed his eyes and looked at me for
a moment. "That's what my tax dollars pay you to do."

One point to The General.

"Now, let's not waste time," he said. "Ask whatever questions you need to ask me to get to the bottom of this mess."

I took a deep breath and regrouped. "Do you know of anyone who wanted to harm your grandson?"

"Money." He leaned forward. "It's the root of all evil. Obviously, someone thought they would get money. It's what motivates people to do all manner of heinous deeds."

I didn't bother to correct his misquotation of the Biblical scripture. Growing up in the church and years of Sunday school on the teachings of Reverend Hilton V. Hamilton brought the correct verse from the sixth chapter, tenth verse of I Timothy to my mind. *For the love of money is the root of all evil.* The General wasn't a man to take kindly to being corrected, so I didn't bother saying it out loud. "My understanding is that Jake didn't have any money."

I saw The General's jaw clench and noticed his right eye twitch. Round two to the St. Joseph Police Department.

"That's true. Jake didn't have any money." He glanced downward and shook his head. "Boy didn't inherit that from me. Must have come from the other side of his family. Killer probably didn't know that. Must have assumed, given his lineage, Jake was loaded."

Now that I mentally calculated we were on equal ground, I was reluctant to rile him up again, so I decided to proceed with caution. "I understand your grandson had a gambling and a drinking problem and that he owed a great deal of money to some…dangerous men."

"Only gambling worthwhile is the stock market."

He looked out the window. After a few moments, he shook his head. "Drinking...another weakness. The only thing worse than a man who can't control his liquor is a woman who can't control her liquor." He continued looking out the window as though we weren't there.

Harley glanced up from his notes. "Did you receive a visit from a man named Mike Maxwell?"

"Small-time hoodlum your lot can't seem to keep behind bars."

Neither Harley nor I rose to the bait and merely sat and waited.

Eventually, The General turned from the window and leaned across the desk. "I wouldn't go as far as to say I 'received' Maxwell. He called several times and even had the nerve to show up unannounced. I refused to receive him. Didn't even bother to return his calls. I can imagine that must have riled someone of his ego." He stopped and looked directly at me. "You're not saying he's the one that killed him, are you?"

I hesitated a few seconds. "It's too early to say. We have no evidence that points directly to one person over another."

He watched me as though he were trying to read my mind.

Harley looked up from his notepad and asked, "Who benefits from Jake's death?"

The General thought for a few moments and then reached down and opened a drawer. He pulled out a manila file folder and placed it on top of the desk. He opened the folder and glanced at the paper inside. "As you already know, my grandson wasn't great with money. When he turned twenty-five, I turned over control of the trust fund I'd set up for him when he was born." He sighed. "Unfortunately, he blew through that money so quickly, it became clear he couldn't be left to manage it himself. So, I froze the small capital he had left and used my lawyers to tie up the money so he wouldn't end up a destitute pauper." He closed the folder and slid it across the desk to me. "I set up a complicated trust that gave him a modest allowance. I hoped he would pull himself together, especially once he married." He shook his head. "Marti had a good head on her shoulders. I hoped she could help him to settle down, but he destroyed that by divorcing her for that little gold digger. Fool couldn't see she was only after his money." He paused and then smiled. "However, I fixed her."

"How'd you do that?" I asked.

"I left the money to his wife." He smiled but saw the puzzled looks on our faces. "His first wife." He laughed. "That little money-grubbing tart won't get a dime of his trust." He leaned back in his chair. "At least I was able to see to that."

The blood drained from Harley's face. "You mean, Marti...ah, his first wife, gets all of his money?"

The General nodded. "I always liked that woman. Good head on her shoulders."

"Surely, his current wife will get something?" Harley said.

"I'm guessing she'll get the money from his insurance policy, if he remembered to change his beneficiary."

We sat for several moments. Harley looked as though he'd just been punched in the gut.

I leaned forward and tried once again to get an answer to the question I'd posed earlier. "Do you know anyone who wanted to see Jake dead?"

"I don't know anyone who hated him that much. Me? I could give you a list a mile long of the men who would dance a jig down Main Street if someone were to punch my clock, but Jake…" For a brief moment, I saw sorrow and sadness flash across his face. "Jake was a fool. He was a weak fool, but I don't know anyone who hated him enough to murder him." The general sat back. Suddenly, he shrank. He leaned forward and placed his elbow on his desk and rested his chin in his hand. The big man looked small and tired.

"We won't keep you any longer," I said, getting to my feet. "But if you think of anything that might help in our investigation, please call me." I placed a business card on his desk, picked up the manila folder and extended my hand.

He looked startled but rose from his seat and shook both of our hands.

"Please accept our sincere condolences."

He swallowed hard and then turned to gaze out of the window.

Harley looked dazed as we walked out into the foyer, but we were both surprised to find Mattie Young waiting at the door with her coat and purse.

"I was hoping I could catch a ride. Mother's Board is meeting tonight, and if I have to wait for the bus, I'll be late."

Harley won a few brownie points by holding the front passenger door open, allowing Sister Young to sit up front, and he climbed into the backseat. He claimed it would be easier since I'd be dropping him off at the precinct on my way.

The ride to the precinct was fairly quiet. Harley was lost in thought, and Sister Young kept her purse close and her mouth closed, apart from a few comments about the unseasonably warm weather and the health of my godmother.

When I stopped to make the turn to the church, Sister Young surprised me by saying, "Ain't you gonna pick up Ella?"

I drove past the church and turned down the alley and made my way to my godmother's house. She was sitting on the porch when we arrived, but she wasn't alone. Sister Green, Chris's grandmother, was there. Dorothea Green was a stocky, older Black woman with kind eyes, a ready smile and a strong, powerful voice. She sang in the senior choir and never failed to bring the church to their feet.

She didn't seem surprised to see either me or Sister Young. She gave us a big smile as we got out of the car.

I gave Mama B a kiss on the cheek, went inside and brought out a couple of extra chairs, passed on the offer for food…for now and then sat down to listen. The women spent several minutes chatting about nothing important, and I zoned out on most of it. My conscious mind registered words like *sugar* and *pressure*. I mentally added the word *blood* in front of both words and gave myself permission to zone out for five minutes longer. Eventually, the conversation got more interesting.

"Dorothea, how's that boy of yours?" Sister Young asked.

Sister Dorothea Green rocked for several moments

with tears streaming down her face. "I don't know. Lord, I just don't know what to do."

It took almost a full sixty-seconds for Mama B and Sister Young to comfort Sister Green so she was no longer sobbing…yes, I counted. Then, it took another five minutes for Sister Young to complete a prayer that had started quietly enough but ended with shouts of praise and thanks to God for resolving the problem, which had yet been voiced. Five minutes was a long time for a prayer, even for the most devout of Christians, which wasn't a label I wore. When the ladies brought their praise down to a low rumble, I slipped a handkerchief into Sister Green's hands. Then, I waited until the lull between the *hallelujahs* and the *praise the lords* was at least thirty seconds.

"Is there anything I can help with?" I asked softly.

Sister Green wiped her eyes. "I came here hoping you'd be here visiting Miss Ella." She sniffed. "I don't know what's wrong with that boy." She shook her head. "He looked me right in the face and lied to me." She shed a few more tears.

"Why don't you tell me what happened?"

She told us about Chris's job working with her sister-in-law Marcia and how he seemed to be doing well.

"Then he just up and quit. He lied and told his aunt he had too much school, but I went to the school today and his teacher said he didn't come." Sister Green pursed her lips. "Apparently, I wrote him a note saying he was sick."

"Lawdy," Sister Young said.

Mama B rocked.

I breathed a sigh of relief. My brain had gone in a

hundred different directions, and I took a moment to bring it back to normal. "Lots of kids play hooky from school." Before the words left my mouth, I knew I was in trouble. Three pairs of eyes glared at me. "I'm not saying it's right, but…"

"Robert James Franklin, Junior." Mama B glared at me. "I know you ain't about to sit there and make excuses for that boy skipping school and telling lies."

The look in Mama B's eyes told me there was only one right answer to that question. "No, ma'am. I'm not but—"

"After everything our people went through to make it possible for young people to get an education, I can't *believe* you're going to sit there and make excuses for him." Sister Young folded her arms across her chest and huffed.

Sister Green leaned forward and pointed the finger of condemnation at me. "I didn't have a choice about going to school. I had to pick cotton in the hot sun from sunup to sundown to put food on the table for my eight sisters and brothers. And do you know how much I made?"

"No, ma'am, but—"

"One dollar per day. For one hundred pounds of cotton. I got one dollar." She huffed.

"But I'm not—"

Sister Young glared at me. "Boy, do you know most families barely made more than one dollar per year for working their fingers to the bone?"

"One dollar was more than I ever got," Mama B said, rocking in her chair. "The plantation owners would send a truck to pick us up during harvest season. We'd all pile in that truck, and he dropped us off in the field and took us home at nightfall. By then, I'd eaten whatever scraps of food I'd brought with me, and I spent what was left in the general store."

Sister Green smiled in remembrance. "Lawd, yes. I remember that truck. We was all piled in them trucks like sardines in a can."

"You were lucky," Sister Young said. "We were share-croppers. In addition to farming our own land, we worked our landlord's land, but no matter how hard you worked, you never got ahead."

"That's because they gave you everything on credit," Sister Green said. "And you'd work and work and never pay it back."

"Gave?" Mama B said and stopped rocking long enough to stare hard at Sister Green. "By the time you paid the interest on the seed and equipment, not to men-tion the lien they put on the crops, you'd be lucky to make enough to buy a loaf of bread." She continued her rocking. "We were blessed to have our own farm, but I had family that sharecropped, and you wanna talk about slavery, that was financial slavery. You were bound to that agreement just as shor' as if you had chains."

I said, "I wasn't trying to belittle—"

"That boy is smart. He has a chance to go to college, and I intend to see to it that he goes, even if it kills him."

I realized nothing I said was going to stop this train, so I sat back and kept quiet.

"It just burns my butt the way young people who have all the advantages in the world just toss it aside," Sister Young said. She took the reassuring nods from her two friends as encouragement to go on. "Take Jake Harrison. That boy had everything. All the best schools his grandfather's money could buy and what did he do? Tossed it away like a dirty tissue on drugs and gambling." She wiped her eyes. "Breaks my heart."

The tongue lashing over, I sat up straight. "Did you say Jake Harrison was taking drugs?"

Sister Young dabbed at her eyes and nodded. "That's why I wanted to get you away. I had a feeling in my bones they wouldn't tell all the truth."

"What's the truth?"

She took several deep breaths, and Sister Green reached across and squeezed her hand until she was composed enough to continue. "His poor mama died giving birth to that baby. She was a good woman, and she wanted that baby so much. Even though the doctors warned her she was too frail…she just wouldn't listen." She sniffed. "Things might have been different if she could have lived. I prayed and prayed. We all did, but… God knows best. I did my best to raise that boy, but nothing can take the place of a mother's love."

"Lawd, don't I know that," Sister Green said. She pulled out her own handkerchief and wiped her eyes. "God knows I've done my best with my boy, but…" Her shoulders shook as she cried over her lost daughter. Eventually, she pulled herself together and remembered Sister Young. "Mattie, I'm sorry. You go ahead and tell RJ what he needs to know."

I nodded a silent thank you and waited.

"When he was little, he was such a sweet boy, always looking for approval from his father and his grandfather, but they was too busy fighting to give two minutes to think about that little boy. The General was too busy making money hand over fist, and his father was too

busy trying to prove he didn't need the General's money."
She paused. "And trying to recover from his wife's death.
He loved that woman with a fierceness that 'bout tore
him apart when she died. He prayed over her like I ain't
never seen nobody pray. It made me think of how when
Jesus was in the garden of Gethsemane and he prayed
until sweat ran down like drops of blood."

Mama B quoted Luke 22:44: *"And being in an agony
he prayed more earnestly: and his sweat was as it were
great drops of blood falling down to the ground."*

"That's it exactly," Sister Young said. "When she
died, something died inside him that day. I think that's
what started him making those...dirty films." She
pursed her lips and shook her head as though to erase
the image of those pictures.

I tried to think of these elderly church matrons
watching Richard Harrison's pornographic movies, but
my imagination wasn't that good.

"Seems to me the trouble with Jake started when
he went away to that expensive boarding school. He
wanted to fit in with the other boys. He had too much
money and no one to give two flying figs what he did.
The only way he could get attention was by acting up.
So, that's what he did. He got kicked out of one boarding school after another." She shook her head. "I tried
to talk The General into letting him stay at home, but
he wouldn't have it."

I appreciated the background, but if Jake Harrison
had been on drugs, then I needed to know. "What about
the drugs?"

"When he came home from college, I noticed a funny
smell in his room. I was cleaning one day and that's

when I found a bag with what looked like herbs in it. I asked him about it, and he just laughed and told me they were special herbs and for me not to worry 'bout it. I showed the bag to his father, and he just laughed, said his boy was sowing his wild oats. But the General flew into a rage and threatened to toss him out if he brought that junk in his home again." She stared at me. "I felt like I was caught between a rock and a hard place. What was I supposed to do? So, I didn't do anything. Was that wrong?"

If anyone understood what it meant to blame yourself for things that were outside of your control, it was me. I told her what the police therapist had told me. "It wasn't your fault. You can't blame yourself for the decisions others make."

Something in her eyes said that she didn't believe me anymore than I had believed the therapist when she had said it to me. We stared at each other, and I knew that we were bound by the chains of guilt. I hoped hers didn't keep her awake at night.

"Anyway, I didn't say anything, but whenever I found the bags in his room, I'd flush them right down the toilet."

I nearly choked. "How did he take that?"

"He got madder than a wet hen, but I didn't care. Then, I started smelling the alcohol on his breath, and his eyes didn't look right to me. They were always bloodshot and half asleep, but then he met Miss Marti." She smiled at the memory. "She reminded me of his young mother, but…she was stronger." She chuckled. "There was nothing frail about her. She was strong inside and out. She had her dog, and she was smart. Jake fell hard for her, just like his dad fell for his mama. Marti didn't care two cents for the General's money, and she didn't have no patience for Richard's nonsense either. When Jake married her, I thought she would whip that boy into shape...but he was weak."

"How did The General feel about her?"

"At first, he thought she was after his money."

"Pshaw," Mama B said. *"The love of money is the root of all evil."*

"I Timothy 6:10," Sister Green said. "And that's shor' 'nuff the truth."

"But Miss Marti showed them. She refused to take any money from them. She had a job, and she refused to marry Jake unless he had a job too. That's when his grandfather set him up in an office of his own at his investment firm. At first, he was doing well. He stopped smelling like a skunk, and I didn't find any more bags of herbs in his room. They got married and bought a house." She pursed her lips. "Not that castle out in the middle of nowhere that he lives in now with... that woman." She paused. "I can't call her his wife. Just because the law says she's his wife and he's living with her...she'll never be his wife in the eyes of God."

Sister Green nodded. "Just like the Samaritan woman that Jesus met at the well. When Jesus asked her to go and call her husband, she had to admit that she didn't have a husband. *Jesus said unto her, Thou hast well said, I have no husband. For thou hast had five husbands; and he whom thou now hast is not thy husband.* John 4:17–18."

"I saw in his eyes, that he knew he'd made a mistake, but...there was no backing out of it. His eyes started looking funny, and his clothes had that smell again." She wrinkled her nose. "I'm sure he was back on *that stuff.*"

"When was the last time you saw him?"

"The day he died. He came to the house. He needed money, as usual." She shook her head. "He pleaded with The General, but he wouldn't give him a dime. Jake stormed out of the house, and that's the last time I saw him alive." She stared in my eyes. "RJ, I need you to catch the person who murdered Jake and make sure they pay for it."

EIGHT

CATCH THE MURDERER and make sure they pay for it. Nothing like a little pressure to get the blood pumping. I pondered Sister Young's statement over and over in my mind. The General failed to mention that he had fought with Jake on the day of his death, but avoidance was another way of dealing with guilt. The General may have been coping with his guilt in Jake's murder in the best way that he knew how. However, as a cop, I needed all of the puzzle pieces to get the full picture and solve a crime, not just the ones people wanted to share.

In true Mama B fashion, she sent me home with a Tupperware container filled with black-eyed peas, candied sweet potatoes and fried chicken. In my heart, I wanted to complain. Mama B needed to watch her cholesterol, and fried chicken wasn't the way to do it, but my stomach had a mind of its own. One whiff of that fried deliciousness and my mouth watered.

I dropped Sister Young off first and then took Sister Green home. After I pulled up, she sat in the car for a few moments.

"I know you're worried about Chris," I said, "and I promise I will talk to him, but I'm going to ask a favor."

She turned to look at me.

"I need you to trust me. Chris is okay. He's just working through some things right now, but he's fine." I couldn't tell her the truth. The last thing Chris needed was Sister Green riding his back and Mike Maxwell filling his mind. "Can you just cut him a little slack and just...trust me."

She stared hard into my eyes, and if I didn't know better, I'd swear she read my soul because she gasped. "He's in trouble, and you know about it. That's why the police have been circling this block like we're running some kind of crack house."

I should have known she'd recognize the extra patrol cars. Little escaped her sight. "He isn't in trouble. He didn't do anything wrong, but he's scared. I just thought a little extra patrol would help to put his mind at ease."

She closed her eyes and took several deep breaths. It didn't take long for her to make up her mind. "Okay. I trust in the Lord." She stared at me. "And I trust you too. Neither of you have failed me yet." She opened the car door, but before she closed the door, she looked at me. "But I'll be relying on you to keep my boy safe, or as God is my witness, I'll hunt you down like a dog and beat the living tar out of you." She slammed the car door.

I drove home wondering what *living tar* was, but I concluded it didn't really matter. It wouldn't be good, whatever it was.

ANOTHER SLEEPLESS NIGHT meant that I was early for work the next morning. Insomnia was hard on the body, but my paperwork had never been so current. However, I could feel the heaviness weighing me down and knew that I only had two good days before I would be forced to resort to pills. I was chugging coffee like a drug addict, caffeine being my drug of choice.

Harley arrived, but before he could even sit down, we received a call from Chief Mike ordering us to meet him at the mayor's office.

Harley and I exchanged glances, but neither of us said anything. While I had been expecting this summons, I'd hoped to have more time.

The mayor's office was located on the top floor of the County-City building, which was just two blocks away. We took the elevator to the twelfth floor, which was high for St. Joseph, and were waved into the office by the mayor's secretary stationed outside his door. Obviously, we were expected. Nevertheless, good manners dictated knocking first. So, we did.

"Come in," Mayor Longbow yelled.

I'd been to Mayor Longbow's office several times, and it never failed to impress. The mayor's office had floor-to-ceiling windows that overlooked the city, large mahogany furniture and plush carpeting that muffled sounds and made you feel like you were stepping on a cloud. In addition to a massive desk, the room was large enough to also hold a conference table and ten chairs. That's where we found the mayor and Chief Mike Barinski waiting.

"Have a seat, gentlemen. I'm on a tight schedule, I wanted to find out where you are with arresting the murderer of Jake Harrison."

Mayor Charles Longbow's office wasn't the only thing that was designed to impress. The mayor himself was also quite distinctive, a fact which he was clearly aware. He was St. Joseph's first Native-American mayor, and he wore his ethnic diversity with pride. He was tall and slender, with dark hair and eyes and brown skin only slightly lighter than my own. As usual, he was immaculately dressed. I was no fashion expert, but even I knew his suits were custom-made and his Italian leather shoes probably cost more than I made in a month. Of course, considering a cop's salary, that wouldn't be hard to do.

Mayor Longbow sat at the head of the table with a nervous Chief Mike to his right. Harley and I sat on his left and declined coffee, although I could feel my hand shake with desire after I smelled the freshly ground beans from the complicated looking contraption that sat near his seat.

"I have a meeting later this afternoon with the General," Mayor Longbow said. He leaned forward and laced his long thin fingers together. "I'll be honest. It's an election year, and I need the General's financial backing. I'd love to be able to tell him we have arrested his grandson's murderer, but Chief Mike here tells me that's not the case." He glared at each of us. "Perhaps you two can fill me in on why not."

Chief Mike never looked comfortable in the mayor's presence, and he tugged at his collar, further wrinkling his already coffee-stained shirt, which Mama B would have described as *rough dried*.

Harley barely spoke in Mayor Longbow's presence, and today was no different. He gave me a sideways glance, which was fine. I was the detective, so it was up to me.

"We haven't arrested a suspect in Jake Harrison's murder because we're still investigating. We have several suspects and want to make sure we don't jump to conclusions."

"Really? I wasn't aware there were so many suspects." Mayor Longbow leaned back in his chair. He gazed at me and then made a motion with his hand as though directing an orchestra, which indicated that I was to proceed.

"There's some evidence that Jake Harrison's ex-wife, Marti Alexander, may have had a motive to kill him. She claimed to have received a text message from the St. Joseph Police Department to show up at the park for a Search and Rescue operation, but we haven't been able to trace that message. However, the current wife, Mrs. Carolyn Harrison, provided an alibi for the ex."

"Wait, the current wife and the ex-wife were together?" Mayor Longbow held up a file folder. "What about the ex-wife's cell phone pinging a tower near the crime scene?"

"We're investigating that. So far, both women claim they were together. We also have reason to believe that Mike Maxwell may be involved."

That got the mayor's attention. "How good of a reason?"

"Jake Harrison had a gambling and an alcohol problem. He may even have been on something stronger than alcohol." Since I'd just learned this last bit the previous night and hadn't had time to update the Chief or Harley, they looked as surprised as the mayor.

"Mike Maxwell claimed Jake Harrison owed him over twenty thousand dollars. Maxwell said he hoped to get his money from the General, but...we only have his word on that."

Mayor Longbow's eyes flashed. "If we could take

down Mike Maxwell, that would be a huge coup for our side." He grinned. "You're going to need to tread very carefully."

Mayor Longbow stood, which signaled the meeting was over, so Chief Mike and Harley rose too, but I wasn't finished. "There's one other suspect."

Mayor Longbow appeared somewhat annoyed but sat back down, as did Chief Mike and Harley.

"When we were at Carolyn Harrison's house, we ran across a car that belonged to Bruce Leonard."

Mayor Longbow narrowed his eyes. "Leonard... Bruce Leonard...why does that name sound familiar?"

Chief Mike cleared his throat and gave the mayor a look. Something passed between the two men during that look that triggered the mayor's memory. "Oh yes, Bruce Leonard. He retired from the police force, right?" He glanced at Chief Mike.

"Yes." Chief Mike tugged at his collar, causing a button to pop off and fly across the table and onto the floor. We didn't attempt to find it.

"Bruce Leonard had a bad reputation when he was a cop," I said, "and I'm not completely sure how he fits into this whole thing, but he was at the Harrisons' house the day we questioned Carolyn Harrison."

Mayor Longbow gave me a long look. "Okay, you have suspects. Investigate, but don't get stuck. Just follow the evidence." He gave me a hard stare which I felt held more meaning than his words, but my lack of caffeine was starting to dull my wits. If there was a message I was supposed to glean, I missed it.

Thankfully, the mayor's phone rang, so we exited.

Chief Mike didn't say anything until we got back to the station, and then he simply held his office door open.

Harley and I entered the cramped space and sat in the two guest chairs and waited. The Chief removed his jacket, sat down, pulled off his tie and tossed it into his desk drawer. "Now, what's all this about Mike Maxwell and twenty thousand dollars?"

I had thought long and hard about how I would divulge the intel on Mike Maxwell without pointing a finger at Chris Green. So, I was ready. Honesty is always the best policy, especially when concealing information from a trained policeman. So, I kept to the truth as much as possible. Jake Harrison's gambling debts were common knowledge. The General told us about Maxwell's attempt to get money, and I even tossed Mattie Young in for good measure. The only part I omitted was anything related to Chris. I knew my confrontation with Maxwell would distract them.

"You actually went to Mike Maxwell's office alone?" Chief Mike boomed. "Have you lost your mind?"

"No, sir. I just thought—"

"You thought?" Chief Mike stood up and paced the few steps allowed in his tiny office. "You want me to believe you thought? Because I seriously doubt that you did. If you'd actually thought this thing through, no way would a highly trained policeman have shown up *alone* in the office of a suspected killer...a man known to be connected to the Chicago mafia. Oh no, you didn't *think*."

Mission accomplished. Chief Mike was too busy reading me the riot act to question where I'd gotten my information. When all else fails, fall on your sword. "I'm sorry, sir."

Chief Mike rubbed his neck. "I don't want you sorry. I want you alive. If you go interviewing Mike Maxwell again *alone*, you're going to be more than *sorry*. You're going to be tied to a desk for the rest of your career. Now, get out there and find who killed Jake Harrison."

I bowed my head and tried to walk, look and act with an appropriate amount of contrition, even though it was taking every bit of strength I had not to jump up and click my heels.

Back at my desk, I poured myself a large cup of coffee, sat down and buried my head in computer work. However, if I thought I was out of the woods, then I was sadly mistaken.

Harley leaned back in his chair and stared at me until I looked up.

"What?"

"You may have fooled Chief Mike, but I know you better than that. You're hiding something."

I didn't insult Harley by denying it, nor did I flatter him by acknowledging it. "We need to talk to Marti Alexander."

Harley didn't say much during our ride. When I rang the doorbell, no one answered. We were about to leave when we heard a lawnmower. We walked around the side of the house. Marti was mowing the grass. She was hot, and her T-shirt and shorts were wet from sweat. She looked up when she saw us and turned off the mower.

"Sorry to interrupt," I said, "but we have a few more questions."

She wiped her forehead with the back of her hand, leaving a streak of dirt. She glanced back at the yard. "I only have a small amount left. Do you mind if I finish?"

We shook our heads.

"It'll just take me a minute. Why don't you two go in the kitchen and pour yourselves some iced tea. I'll join you in five minutes."

Inside, we were greeted by Callie, who sniffed me. Then, she stood up on her back legs, put her front paws on Harley's shoulders and licked him as though he were covered in bacon.

Harley gave me a look that said *Help me*, but I took a sip of tea and left him to fend for himself.

In less than five minutes, Marti came inside, took one glance at Callie and Harley and said, "Callie, off."

The standard poodle reluctantly removed her paws, but she kept her eyes glued to my partner.

Marti wiped her forehead and neck with a paper towel. "I'm sorry about the delay, but I needed to get that done before it got really hot and I knew if I stopped, I'd never go back out there."

The kitchen was small but sunny and bright, with white cabinets and a small bistro table with two chairs near a bay window that overlooked the backyard. Harley stood up to offer her his seat but was waved back down by Marti. "Please, don't get up. I'm hot, sweaty and covered in grime and grass clippings. If I sit down now, you'll never be able to pry me out of that chair."

Harley didn't like it, but he returned to his seat. Callie put her head in his lap and looked up into his face with a look of pure adoration. He reached out and scratched her ear and smiled.

"Please, ask me whatever questions you want," Marti said.

I glanced at Harley to make sure he had taken out his notepad and pen. "Have you been able to think of anything else that might be helpful in the investigation?"

She leaned against the counter and took a long drink of tea. "No. Any luck with the text message?"

"I wouldn't hold out much hope there. Whoever sent you that message to come to the river probably used a burner phone."

She rubbed small circles on her temples. "Sorry, I have an awful headache. What did you want to ask me?"

"Why didn't you tell us that you stood to inherit from Jake's death?"

She stared at me as though I had suddenly grown another head. "What are you talking about?"

"According to The General, Jake's trust names you as the beneficiary." I gave her a hard stare. "Are you saying you didn't know?"

"I knew that he listed me the beneficiary when Jake and I were married, but…we're not married anymore. We're divorced. I made it very clear to Jake that I didn't want anything from him. I refused alimony. I… I assumed when he remarried, he would change all of that. That should go to Caroline. She's his wife now." She looked from me to Harley and back again. "Are you telling me that no one bothered to change the beneficiary?"

"That's what The General told me. Although, he thinks she may benefit from his life insurance…if Jake remembered to change that."

The temple circles increased. "Oh, God. Jake was horrible with money. I doubt if he would have bothered, but surely Caroline would have reminded him."

I could tell by the shock reflected in her eyes when the point of my question finally hit home. She stood up straight. "Wait, are you telling me that because he didn't change the papers, that I will inherit Jake's trust fund?"

I nodded.

"That can't be. Surely, that's not legal. I'm not his wife anymore. That money should all go to Caroline, not me. I don't want it. I told him that. When I left, I told him I didn't want anything from him, especially not money."

"Why not?" Harley asked.

"It says in the Bible, *The love of money is the root of all evil.* Well, I believe it. Money was the driving force in that family. The General was so obsessed with making money that he couldn't be bothered with his son or his grandson. He has more money than he could ever spend, but he just keeps on making more and more. I think that's why Richard turned to...well, the lifestyle that he did. He wanted to get more money than his father and rub his nose in it. Neither one of them stopped to think about Jake and what this was doing to him." She paused and then shook the memories out of her head. "They used money to control Jake and he wasn't strong enough to see what they were doing. He wasn't strong enough to tell them to take their money and shove it. Money made him weak." A look of panic crossed her face. "I don't have to take it, do I?"

"You can probably decline the money, but are you sure you want to do that?" I tried to imagine turning down that much money, but my imagination wasn't that good. "You'll be a millionaire. You could have a bigger kennel and dog training franchise."

She shook her head. "I don't want or need a bigger kennel or dog training business. I gave away my other dogs after Callie's last litter to a good breeder. They'll be well taken care of, and now it's just me and Callie. We don't need much, and we're happy."

"Money can be used to do good too," Harley said, his face flushed. "You could start a charity or give money to the ASPCA or a dog rescue. Not all rich people are evil." Perhaps he was thinking about his own trust fund, which his family had accumulated from their plantations several hundred years ago.

Marti squeezed the back of her neck. "That much money is a big responsibility. I can't take the risk that I won't let it corrupt me. No, I don't want it, and I'm pretty sure they can't make me take it. I'll get an attorney if I have to."

Marti looked ready to fall over, so we thanked her for the tea and made our exit. On the ride home, Harley asked, "Do you believe that she didn't know about the money?"

I thought about it. "Yeah. I don't think she had a clue."

"Me either."

"Of course, it doesn't matter what you or I believe. If this comes to court, the only opinions that will matter will be the twelve jurors who will decide her fate."

At the precinct, Harley looked as though he wanted to ask questions, but he didn't. I could tell he knew I was holding something back. However, we'd worked together long enough that he knew I'd tell him if I could.

At least, I hoped he knew it. Regardless, he didn't push, and for that I was grateful.

I stayed busy until noon, and then I told Harley I needed to run an errand. I could tell by his smile and sly expression that he thought I was going to meet Paris. I let him think it.

I stopped at a nearby convenience store and then drove to River Bend High School and hurried to the office. Chris Green had missed one day of school, and I was taking a chance he wouldn't miss two in a row. Actually, I was making a calculated assumption that his grandmother would see to it he didn't miss two days in a row, even if it meant she had to walk him to school and sit in the classroom to ensure he stayed. I was rewarded when I learned he had been checked as present, and a messenger was sent with a note asking Chris to come to the office.

I didn't have long to wait, but I felt a pang of guilt when I saw the look of sheer terror in Chris's eyes as he slowly crept toward the office.

"Man, RJ, you 'bout gave me a heart attack."

"Sorry." I glanced around and escorted him outside. "You got time for lunch?"

"With you? Absolutely, but I gotta be back in forty-five minutes or my grandmother will skin me alive."

I grinned, and we hurried to my car. There was a fast food burger joint nearby, but experience had taught me the line would take all of Chris's forty-five minutes. So, I took a few side streets and made my way to a small café which was too far for students to walk but close enough that I knew we would easily be able to grab food and get back in time.

St. Joseph Café was a small diner that looked like a dive, but it actually had some of the best hamburgers in town. Inside, we quickly found a seat near the back and ordered burgers, fries and shakes.

"Your grandmother was worried."

He hung his head. "I know."

"I thought we agreed you would continue as usual. Go to school. Go to work. Don't say or do anything to draw attention to yourself."

"I know, but… I got scared."

"Why? Did Mike Maxwell—"

"No, I don't know why I did it. I just spent the entire night working myself up, and next thing I knew, I was jumping at my own shadow. Man, a cat crossed the yard and I 'bout wet my pants."

I had to force myself not to laugh. Admitting he'd been that frightened took a lot of courage. Thankfully, our food arrived and gave me something else to focus on.

We ate in silence for a few moments.

"No one knows what you saw," I said. "I haven't told anyone."

He slowed down shoveling the fries in his mouth and nodded. "I know. Plus, I saw the patrol cars around the house." He looked up. "That was you, right?"

"There's extra patrols around the school and your house, but it probably wouldn't hurt if we had some type of…safe word. You know what that is?"

"Yeah. If I need help, I can say it without anyone knowing, and you'll come get me."

"Right, so whaddya think?"

He took another bite of his burger. "Okay, what?"

"Is Mr. Freemont still teaching French?"

He frowned. "Yeah, but I'm taking Spanish, not French."

"Great. So, if you call and say you left your French book in my car with your homework and you need me to bring it you, then few people would know, right?"

"I guess so."

I reached in my pocket and pulled out the phone I'd bought earlier at the convenience store and passed it across. "Take this. It's a phone with prepaid minutes." He reached for the phone, but I kept a hand on it, preventing him from taking it. "This isn't for talking to your friends or your girlfriend. This is just for emergencies. You got it?"

"Got it."

"I turned on location tracking and downloaded an app that will let me find you wherever you are. If you call me from that phone, then I'll get to you. If you can't call me, just make sure the phone is turned on, and I'll get to you."

Chris examined the phone for a few moments. He made a few swipes on the phone and held it up. "Smile, RJ."

"I'm going to need you to take this seriously."

He made a swipe that must have reversed the camera to selfie mode. "And there you have Detective RJ Franklin, seeker of justice and killer of fun." He stopped the recording and slid the phone into his pocket. He grinned. "Thanks."

We finished eating, and I drove him back to school with plenty of time for him to get to his next class. He hopped out of the car and slammed the door. "Thanks for lunch." He ran a few steps and then turned and ran back to the car.

I rolled down the window on the passenger side.

He stuck his head inside. "Thanks for everything, RJ."

We knuckle punched. His shoulders relaxed, and when he ran inside the building, there was a lightness in his step that released the vice grip on my chest the slightest bit.

I WALKED BACK into the office, and Harley's face screamed an accusation, *WHERE WERE YOU?* I ignored his face and concentrated on bracing myself for whatever new ordeal had arisen in the hour and a half that I'd been gone.

Harley dropped a report on my desk, which I could clearly see contained the forensic and trace evidence report for the Harrison murder.

I scanned the file for whatever item had gotten my partner's blood pressure up. One of Marti's hairs was found on the body, which didn't prove anything. She was at the scene. She found the body. A good attorney wouldn't have a problem explaining that. However, the item that had most likely gotten Harley riled up was that a secondary sweep of the area had found a gun— Marti's gun, which ballistics had confirmed was the murder weapon.

NINE

"SHE DIDN'T DO IT. No way would she be stupid enough to use her own gun to murder her ex-husband and then leave the gun at the crime scene." Harley paced a circle around my desk. "She could have tossed that gun in the river. Why leave it at the crime scene where she has to know it would be found?"

I leaned back in my chair. "The district attorney will say she and Jake fought. She had the gun in her pocket, and in a fit of rage, she shot him. Once she realized what she'd done, she panicked and dropped it."

We'd both seen that scenario too many times to push it away too quickly, but I could see the gears inside his head turning as he revved up for another defense.

I was so engrossed in the file and watching Harley's emotional roller coaster, I didn't see Tim Austen, the assistant district attorney, arrive until he spoke.

"Or maybe she was counting on her police friends thinking she was too smart to leave her gun at the crime scene," Tim said, perching on the corner of my desk.

Blond hair, blue eyes, with teeth worthy of a toothpaste commercial, Tim looked like a pampered rich kid who spent his summers yachting and playing polo, which he was. However, there was more to him than met the eye. Despite the fact that he was the only son of one of St. Joe's upper-crust families, he was also smart and hardworking, with a reputation for always being fair.

"She couldn't know we'd think that," Harley said.

Tim winked. "If I didn't know better, I'd think our little friend here is smitten."

"I'm just trying to be thorough. My gut tells me she didn't do it."

"Your gut?" Tim glanced at me. "Since when has the St. Joseph Police Department been using gut-evidence as an investigative technique?"

"What brings you here?" I said. "Slumming?"

"Maybe I'm just checking to see if you're ready for that rematch." He grinned and mimicked shooting a basketball.

Tim had a good jump shot, which he'd used to defeat me the last time we'd gone one on one at the gym. However, since my accident, basketball, like sleep, had gone by the wayside. Every baller knew that basketball was ten percent skill and ninety percent getting into your opponent's head.

I glanced around. "You can't be talking to me? Didn't you hear, I got a new job?"

He narrowed his eyes, but after a long pause, he asked, "What job?"

"I'm the new bus driver. I take Wanna-Be-Ballers like you to school." I laughed.

"That's lame, old man. I was going to take it easy on you since I heard you got banged up, but obviously there's nothing wrong with your mouth."

I rubbed my back. "Actually, I have been having some back pains."

Tim looked suspicious but eventually asked, "Okay, how'd you hurt your back?"

I waited a few beats. "Carrying you through the All-City Basketball Tournament."

Tim had a good sense of humor, and we passed a few more barbs back and forth before settling down to business. "Can we talk?"

I knew Tim wanted a private conversation, so I got up and walked with him out to his car. He didn't say anything until we were alone outside. "I'm hearing a lot of talk about this case."

I folded my arms and waited.

"The General isn't just a rich man. He's rich and very connected." He gave me a look that held a warning. Without saying a word, I knew that if I didn't make an arrest soon, I'd be sacrificed to appease The General's feelings, the mayor's political aspirations and the department's reputation.

"How much time do I have?"

"Probably a couple of days, no more." He unlocked the car and put his briefcase inside. "You wouldn't have that much if the mayor wasn't envisioning the possibility of walking out for a press conference to announce that he'd taken down a member of the mafia." He climbed behind the wheel, started the engine and rolled down the driver's side window. "I'm not sure what you have on Mike Maxwell, but…be careful."

I watched as Tim backed out of the parking lot and drove away.

That weight that had lifted temporarily when I'd left Chris at school was firmly back in full force, along with a couple extra pounds of pressure for good measure.

I needed to think. I glanced at my watch. Instead of heading back inside, I got in my car and headed downtown.

One of Paris's two salons was located downtown in the old Fullers Building. The warehouse had once been the home of Fullers Cheese manufacturing, but in the eighties, the factory closed and moved all operations to Wisconsin. The warehouse now held retail stores, specialty shops and a restaurant.

Paris's salon, *Un jour à Paris*, was on the lower level. I didn't know French, but I knew from asking that it meant *A Day in Paris*. She'd decorated the lower level to look like a Paris street with wallpaper that included the Eiffel Tower, the Arc de Triumph and the Notre-Dame de Paris.

Inside, the décor was high-end, with plush carpeting, soft music and dim lights.

"Bonjour, RJ." Paris's receptionist, Amy, flashed me an enthusiastic smile. "I'll bet you're here to see Paris. Let me see if she is free." Amy was seventy-five and perpetually happy. She had an eclectic style that was reflected in her wardrobe, which always included a red hat, as well as a genuine zest for life that was infectious. She picked up a telephone and relayed the information. When she hung up, she smiled again. "She'll be right up."

Amy was also addicted to sweets. She held up a candy dish like a pusher offering me my first taste of illegal drugs. "Would you like some candy?"

I declined.

It didn't take long for Paris to come out to greet me. Today, she had her braids pulled up into an elaborate

bun. She was dressed all in black. Black pants, black shirt
and a long bright pink scarf wrapped around her neck.
She smiled and walked up and gave me a kiss, which left
no doubt that she was, indeed, glad to see me.

"Are you here to take me for a tea break?"

Paris was a busy businesswoman with two hair salons. She was renovating her house, sang in the church
choir and was currently helping with the children's choir
while the church looked for a new Minister of Music,
after our last one was murdered. Despite her busy lifestyle, she made time for herself by taking a break for tea
each afternoon.

"Absolutely."

She turned back to Amy, "I'll be back in about an
hour."

"Take your time."

Paris and I walked the short distance from her salon
to her favorite shop for afternoon tea, The River Bend
Chocolate Factor was a franchise that had been started
by some former MACU students and was now thriving
with shops throughout Indiana and Southwestern Michi-
gan. Paris found a seat while I ordered. Even though the
shop was busy, it didn't take long for them to prepare
our tea and scones.

When I came out, I spotted Paris seated at a small
bistro table near the window. She gazed out onto the
sun-soaked patio at two birds enjoying the remains of
a half-eaten croissant someone had left for their enjoy-
ment. I balanced our tray while Paris removed our mugs
and the scone I'd ordered for her.

We sipped our tea in a companionable silence. After

a few moments, she asked, "You gonna tell me what's bothering you?"

"What makes you think anything's bothering me? Maybe I just wanted to enjoy a few moments with the prettiest girl in St. Joe."

"Ha! As much as I would love to believe you, I can see in your eyes that something's bothering you." She sipped her tea. "It's okay if you don't want to talk. I'm fine just enjoying tea with the handsomest guy in St. Joe."

I took a sip of my tea. Normally, talking to Paris helped me put things in perspective and clear my mind. However, normally my girlfriend didn't know the people involved. The police's number one suspect was her dog trainer and friend. I trusted Paris, but would she be able to keep from telling Sister Green that Chris could potentially be in danger if she knew about what he'd heard from Mike Maxwell? I believed she would, but it was a tough burden to carry.

She reached across the table and squeezed my hand. "RJ, I hope you know I'd never willingly betray any confidence you choose to share with me, right?"

"I know, it's just…this is different."

"Okay, then why don't you just tell me the parts that you can. Don't worry about it making sense."

I didn't think that was going to work, but I figured I had nothing to lose. Without giving out names, I told her that there was someone who had information that might be helpful in a case I was working, but the person was afraid to come forward. I told her that without this information, I might never get the person, but that I didn't feel right pressuring them to come forward. I talked about the pressure to arrest someone on one of my cases even though I wasn't confident that the person actually committed the murder. Lastly, I told her that if I failed, then I would most likely be fired.

She listened intently. When I finished, she said, "I don't know anything about being a policeman, but I do know that you're good at your job. You care about the law and you care about people."

"Thanks," I said. "I appreciate that completely biased assessment."

"You know what you're doing. If you didn't feel comfortable pressuring someone to come forward, then you must have had a good reason for it. I don't know if it was your instinct or what Reverend Hamilton would call the guidance of the Holy Spirit. Regardless..." She waved her hand. "It doesn't matter the reason. Something guided you to do what you did, and I think you just need to trust your instincts."

"What if my instincts were guided by my personal feelings?"

"Why does that make it wrong?" She stared at me, but I didn't have an answer. "You'll catch the murderer. You always do, but if by some bizarre twist of fate you don't...so what?"

"I could get fired."

"I seriously doubt it. Let's face facts. St. Joe is rather short on experienced detectives, but let's suppose you did...you have other options. You could teach or be a police consultant or open your own detective agency or...you could make furniture in your garage."

When the shock of her statement wore off, I realized she was right. I'd been offered the opportunity to consult after my accident. Judge Browning wanted me to teach another class at MACU. I had my townhouse and a little money in the bank. I wouldn't starve, nor would I be homeless.

"You're right." I grinned. "Who knows? I might just enjoy making furniture in my garage."

She smiled. "As long as you finish the console table for my front entry first, then go for it."

We finished tea, and I walked Paris back to her salon. When we arrived, her next customer was waiting.

"Mrs. Anderson, why don't you go back to my chair," Paris said. "I'll be right back."

A well-preserved, gray-haired older woman smiled and headed around the corner.

Paris turned back to me. "Are we still on for dinner tonight?"

"Cesselly's?" Cesselly's was owned by former jazz musicians and featured live music. It also happened to be Paris's favorite restaurant.

"You know what I like." She reached up and kissed me goodbye. "I'll see you later."

I turned to leave, but she grabbed my sleeve. When I turned around, she took my face in her hands and stared hard into my eyes. "Be careful." When I nodded, she reached up and kissed me hard, then released me, turned and walked away.

My Lord, He calls me
He calls me by the thunder
The trumpet sounds within-a my soul
I ain't got long to stay here

TEN

WITH PARIS'S CAUTION floating through my head, I drove
back to the precinct determined to do what I needed
to do. I walked in and found Harley where I'd left him
over an hour earlier.

"We need a warrant to search Marti Alexander's
house."

I could see his words about to bubble to the surface,
but I held up a hand to stop them. "Look, I didn't say
an *arrest* warrant. I said a *search* warrant. I know you
don't think she did it…and maybe I don't think so either. The bottom line is we have a job to do, and we're
going to do it based on facts. Maybe the search will
prove she couldn't possibly have killed her ex-husband.
Either way, we do our job." I looked him in the eyes.
"If you don't feel able to do your job, just say the word,
and I'll have someone else assigned."

Harley's chest heaved, but he must have realized it
was in his best interest to stay assigned to the case. He
took a few slow deep breaths and nodded.

I completed the necessary paperwork for the search
warrant. In bigger cities, getting a judge to review and
sign a warrant could take days. St. Joe was small enough
that I knew I'd have my warrant in a few hours.

Chief Mike was ecstatic to see progress, but he agreed that we should wait until Thursday to execute it. I felt a tug of sympathy at the slump in Harley's shoulders as he pored over files and reports. However, I knew he'd get over it. In fact, it might help spur him on to find evidence that would lead to another suspect.

"You staying late?" I asked before leaving to go home to shower and change for my date.

"Yeah, I just want to go back through everything again."

I grinned as I left.

SEVERAL YEARS AGO, a developer had started construction on a row of townhouses built to resemble a converted warehouse in a neighborhood of traditional residential homes. The complex was contemporary with great views of the St. Thomas River. When the developer filed bankruptcy, the bank foreclosed. Fortunately, banks are rarely interested in owning real estate. My realtor said it was easier to sell the units individually rather than looking for someone to buy the entire complex. I managed to get an end unit for one-third of the appraised value, which made it affordable, even on a cop's salary.

Three stories, brick walls, seventeen-foot ceilings, exposed pipes, minimalist modern furniture and outstanding river views were appealing. The oversized two-car garage underneath was what sold me. I carved out a small amount of space for a wood shop. It wasn't big enough to make furniture…well, not a lot of it anyway. However, I enjoyed my Zen-like retreat.

I showered and changed into black jeans with a black cashmere sweater that Paris had bought me for a nothing-special-just-saw-it-on-sale-and-thought-of-you gift. She and Mama B were great at those. Thoughts of Mama B sent me into the kitchen, where I collected all of the Tupperware I'd taken home for the week.

WHEN I ARRIVED at Paris's house, I knew from the look on her face that all was not right in her world. "What's wrong?"

She scowled. "That dog hates me."

I made sure not to show the slightest frown. "What did she do?"

Paris beckoned me to follow her to the laundry room where Maya stayed during the day. The normally immaculate room looked as though it had snowed inside. There was white fluff and bits of foam everywhere. Like all cops, I was trained to notice things. I noticed the dog bed, which used to sit in the corner, was missing. I also noticed that the fluff and foam covering the floor also hung from Maya's mouth.

Paris spread her arms wide to encompass the total situation, dog and room. "After an entire day on my feet, I came home to this."

"Come here." I pulled her into my embrace and held her for a few moments. "Why don't we skip going out tonight? You look like you need a break."

She glanced up at me. "I still need to eat, and you look nice." She sniffed. "You smell nice too." She smiled and snuggled close. "I haven't even had time to take a shower and change."

"Why don't you go upstairs and take a nice long bubble bath. I'll clean this up and take Maya for a little

ride. We'll pick up Chinese takeout." I glanced around.
"I can even pick up a new dog bed."

"That sounds wonderful. Are you sure?"

"Absolutely."

She was tired and didn't take much convincing. I put
Maya outside while I swept up the remains of the great
dog bed attack. Then, I put on her leash and headed out
to my car with the still unrepentant poodle.

My first stop was to a big box pet store. The beauty
of pet stores was they allowed you to bring your four-
legged friends inside. I'd learned from previous visits
with Paris that this made it easier when choosing col-
lars or other canine accoutrements. Maya and I walked
inside, where she was immediately pounced on by two
small children who asked to pet her. Five minutes later,
Maya had licked the children clean, and they had to
be carried out kicking and screaming by their parents.

We found a bountiful supply of dog beds in a variety of colors, sizes and materials. After glancing at a
large wall that was filled from floor to ceiling, I was…
overwhelmed. However, a blue-shirted salesclerk must
have noticed the confused look on my face and took pity
on me. When I explained the foam dog bed battle, he
walked me down the aisle. Here, he pointed out an attractive bed which was large, covered in a dark-washed
denim and filled with recyclable plastic bottles. I must
have looked suspicious because he assured me the fill
was comfortable and the tough denim covering would
withstand Maya's razor-sharp puppy teeth.

We put the bed on the ground, and Maya sniffed it.
She walked on it. And, eventually, she sat down beside it.

I wasn't sure until my blue-shirted salesclerk told me the cover was removable for easy cleaning, or the entire bed could be tossed in the washer if needed. That's when I was sold. It was a bit pricier than some of the other dog beds, but I figured it was worth it to save over one hundred plastic water bottles from a landfill. Not to mention saving my girlfriend's sanity.

Of course, we didn't make it out of the store with just a dog bed. Maya took a detour down the toy aisle, and I picked up a white lamb that looked like Lamb Chop from a show I remembered from my childhood that featured ventriloquist Shari Lewis. I made the mistake of giving the Lamb Chop toy to Maya, and then she didn't want to let it go. At the register, we had a brief tug-of-war, but the cashier simply bent over and used a handheld scanner to ring up the toy, which was still in Maya's mouth.

I put the dog bed in the backseat, and Maya climbed in without ever dropping her new toy. The Tupperware on the seat reminded me that I had another stop to make. So, Maya and I drove over to the southeast side of town to Mama B's house.

I had a feeling how this was going to go down, but I didn't want to assume anything. I pulled up in front of Mama B's house and rolled down the windows, grabbed the Tupperware and got out.

"Maya, stay!"

She stayed. The car door was closed, so she didn't have much choice. However, she didn't stay quietly. In fact, from the moment I got out, she barked.

I knocked on the front door and was ordered to come in, the door was open.

Inside, I found Mama B in her normal position, rocking in her recliner, watching Columbo on television.

I kissed her cheek and held up the Tupperware.

"You can put that in the kitchen and then go and bring in that dog so I can meet her."

I had a feeling she would want me to bring her inside, but I wasn't sure Maya was up to this meeting. Nevertheless, I did as instructed.

I put Maya's leash on, and she hopped out of the car, still holding her toy. I walked her to a small grassy area to the side of the house, and she squatted and took care of business without releasing her grip on her toy. When she was done, she and Lamb Chop pranced up the porch stairs and walked into Mama B's front room.

Mama B stopped rocking long enough to make eye contact with her. Mama B stared into Maya's soul, and something passed between them. For several moments, nothing happened. Then, Maya's tail began to wag.

"Maya, come." Mama B patted her lap and Maya opened her mouth, dropped her toy and took a flying leap into Mama B's lap.

"Good girl." Mama B scratched her ear, and Maya's eyes rolled back into her head. She looked as though she was going to pass out.

Mama B unsnapped her leash and dropped it on the floor. Then, she and Maya curled up and watched Columbo.

Mama B scratched Maya until she fell asleep. "Where's Paris? Isn't tonight your normal date night?"

"She had a rough day and was tired, so we're giving her a little break. I'm going to pick up Chinese food for dinner."

"Pshaw. I don't know nothin' 'bout no China food, but I got some collard greens, fried corn and smothered steak in the fridge."

I knew Paris well enough to know that given a choice between any takeout and something homemade by Mama B, she would opt for Mama B's food. Nevertheless, I sent her a text message anyway. Her response was pretty much what I expected, YOU HAD ME AT FRIED CORN. TELL MAMA B, THANK YOU. Since I had my cell phone out, I snapped a picture of Maya curled up with Mama B in her recliner and sent that.

Paris's response was a series of emoji's that ranged from shock to laughter and ended with a series of hearts.

"You figure out what's keeping you awake at night yet?" Mama B said.

"I'm a cop with a backlog of cases. My boss thinks my girlfriend's dog trainer killed her ex-husband. My girlfriend doesn't and wants me to prove it. My partner has been bewitched by the dog trainer and *thinks* he's in love. It's an election year, and the mayor wants a quick arrest so he can get a hefty campaign endorsement. I have a kid scared out of his mind because he may be a target of a former mafia thug. And every time I close my eyes for more than five minutes, I see the face of a little girl who I wasn't able to save."

I heard snoring coming from the recliner and looked over to see that Maya was using Mama B's leg as a pillow and was curled up and sound asleep. Mama B glanced down at the snoring dog and smiled. "Sounds like you got a lot of things to sort out, but I don't think those are the problems keeping you up at night. You've had almost all of those same problems before."

"Maybe you could give me a clue what you think it is. I could use all the help I can get."

She chuckled at something on the television. "Do you think the dog trainer killed her ex-husband?"

I didn't even need to think about it. "No."

"Then, that ain't it."

I laughed. "Just because I don't think she did it, doesn't mean I'm right." I rubbed the crick that had settled into the back of my neck. "Even if I am right, it doesn't guarantee that she won't get arrested for murder anyway. If I don't make an arrest, the chief will just assign the case to someone else who will arrest her."

She waved her hand. "You'll find the killer. I'm not worried about that, but you need to get some sleep or you'll likely make a mistake that could cost you more than a few hours' sleep."

She was right. I could feel the weariness settle over my body. My brain felt like it was trapped in a fog. I stood up and stretched. "I better get Maya home or Paris will be worried."

Maya opened her eyes and lifted her head at the sound of her name, but she didn't move.

"I made my grandfather's tonic to help you sleep. It's curing on the ledge on the back porch."

I stared. "What kind of tonic?"

She continued to watch Columbo. "It's in a mason jar. Drink it before you go to bed."

I went in the kitchen and packed up the Tupperware for Paris and my dinner. I checked the back porch and saw a jar with a clear liquid sitting on the window ledge. I held it up to the light, but it looked like water. I added it to the bag. Back in the living room, I called Maya.

She looked at me but refused to move.

Mama B's lips twitched, but after a few moments, she said, "Maya, I appreciate you coming and cuddling up with an old woman, but it's time for you to go home now."

Maya looked at her, stood up and hopped out of the chair. She stretched and then moved in front of me.

"Oh, you ready to come with me now?" I said.

Maya wagged her tail. She picked up her Lamb Chop toy from where she had left it on the floor and allowed me to snap on her leash.

I kissed Mama B, and we headed outside.

"You take that tonic before you go to bed. It'll help you sleep."

"Okay."

"And don't forget to bring back my good Tupperware."

When I got back to Paris's house, she was in a better mood. She had set the table, dimmed the lights and had a bottle of wine chilling and soft jazz playing.

She loved the dog bed, and Maya was fond of it too. While Paris and I ate, Maya curled up in her bed. She used her Lamb Chop toy for a pillow and finished the nap she had started at Mama B's house.

Paris glanced over at her curled up in her bed. "She looks so cute when she sleeps. It's hard to stay angry at her when I see her like that."

"It was weird. Mama B stared in her eyes like, *I'm the top dog in this house.* I think she hypnotized her."

Paris laughed. "Well, if that's all it took to turn her from the Tasmanian Devil that ripped up dog beds, to that—" she pointed at the sleeping dog "—then, she can hypnotize her every day of the week."

We ate. We talked and sipped wine. When we were done eating, we moved into the living room and cuddled up. I knew our romantic evening would end early when Paris yawned the second time. She was asleep within thirty minutes.

Careful not to wake her, I extracted myself. I covered her with a throw, grabbed my mason jar and Mama B's Tupperware and made a speedy and silent exit.

At home, I took a shower and got ready for bed. I carefully unscrewed the lid of the mason jar and took a whiff. The aroma made my eyes water and my nose burn. I took a small sip from the jar and broke into a coughing fit that left me wheezing and leaning over the sink.

I pulled out my cell phone and dialed Mama B. When she picked up, I launched into my attack. "Were you deliberately trying to kill me? What exactly is in that… tonic?"

She chuckled. "It's my grandfather's secret recipe."

"You never told me your grandfather made moonshine."

"You never asked."

I didn't have to see her to know that she was smiling. I could hear it in her voice. "Seriously, what's in this stuff? Because I'm pretty sure I tasted gasoline and tar."

"It's a secret. If I told you what was in it, I'd have to kill you."

"Is this stuff legal? Where on earth are you hiding your still?"

"Boy, you ask way too many questions. You just drink some of that and it'll cure whatever ails you."

"If I drank that jar, I'd be knocked out for a week."

"At least you'd get a good sleep." She laughed. "Now,

take the tonic and get you some sleep." She hung up the phone.

I stared at the cell phone and then took another look at my mason jar of death. *If Mama B can take this stuff, then I can too.* I held my nose and took a long gulp. I felt like my throat was on fire, but I swallowed and prayed it wouldn't eat through my stomach lining. When my eyes finally stopped watering and I was able to walk, I stood up, screwed the top back on the toxic sludge and put it in the pantry.

I turned on a basketball game and got in bed. One of the West Coast teams was introducing their starting lineup. The next thing I knew, my cell phone was ringing. I wiped the drool from my mouth, reached over and grabbed the phone. "Hello?"

"RJ, are you coming in? We have the warrant to search Marti's house, and I was hoping we could talk before we went over there."

"What time is it?"

Harley paused. "It's eight fifteen."

Hearing the time was like a dose of cold water. I forced myself to sit up. "I'll be there in thirty minutes."

I can't remember the last time I slept through the night without waking up in a cold sweat. My throat was sore, and my tongue felt like sandpaper. Other than that, I felt fine.

I took a quick shower, dressed and rushed out the door. I made a mental note to thank Mama B. The swill she'd mixed up gave me the first good night's sleep I'd had in quite some time.

Harley was waiting for me at the precinct. He handed

me the warrant, but I could tell by the way he avoided making eye contact that something was bothering him.

"Can we talk…some place… I mean this is—"

"I could use a donut and some coffee. Let's walk over to Adamo's Bakery."

We made the short trek to the bakery, ordered coffee and donuts and then found a table in a quiet corner.

I ate two glazed donuts before Harley worked up the nerve to talk.

"I have to take myself off the case."

"Okay." The slump of his shoulders indicated that there was more behind this, so I waited.

"Last night, I…went out with her."

I put the donut down and glared. "You what?"

He held up his hands to fend off my attack. "I know… I know I shouldn't have gone, but… I was sitting at my desk when Sir Percy came by. He saw me sitting there and invited me to go eat."

I took a deep breath. "So, you weren't alone with her. Sir Percy was with you?"

He squirmed. "He was in the beginning." I started to talk, but he hurried on. "Look, it'll be faster if you just let me tell you what happened."

I nodded.

He took a deep breath. "So, Sir Percy and I went to the Hair of the Dog."

The Hair of the Dog was an English pub located downtown. They served Americanized British cuisine, and I knew it was a favorite of Sir Percy's. "Okay."

"We had a few drinks, and he got a call. It was Marti. I heard him invite her to join us, and she must have said yes, because within fifteen minutes, there she was." He took a deep breath. "We talked about England and dogs. Then, Sir Percy got a call and said he had to go back to work. He asked me to see that his niece got home safely." Harley's eyes pleaded with me. "I said I would, so I followed her home. I had every intention of just seeing her to her door and then leaving, but…she invited me inside, and I went." He bowed his head.

I felt the knot develop in the back of my neck. My shoulders rose, and my neck shrank down. Twisting my head in circles failed to raise my neck, lower my shoulders or eliminate the knot.

"RJ, I swear to you, nothing happened. We just talked. That's all."

"What did you talk about? The case? The fact that we had a search warrant and planned to search her house today?"

A spark of anger flashed across his face, but the look in my eyes must have been enough to douse it. He released a breath and shook his head. "I suppose I deserve that, but the answer's NO. No, I didn't talk about the case. I didn't talk about the search warrant, and I never talked about anything connected to the case."

I searched his eyes, but I didn't see anything that led me to doubt the sincerity of his words. Nevertheless, this was beyond inappropriate. "Was this part of a plan?"

He frowned. "What do you mean?"

"Was this your way of getting her off? Because you know if we arrest her, and it comes out that you were… having a sexual relationship with her, then her lawyer can throw out the case."

He shoved his chair back and leapt to his feet. His thrust out his chest.

I leapt to my feet. I put my face within inches of his and stared into his eyes. "Seriously, you wanna go there with me?"

He glared, but I watched as the fuel that had propelled him just moments earlier slowly seeped out of his body. When the last bits left, he flopped back down into his seat.

I glanced around at the suddenly quiet bakery and saw that all eyes were fixed on us. I took a deep breath and returned to my seat, and the restaurant noise returned to its previous levels.

"Did you sleep with her?"

He swallowed hard. "No."

"Did you discuss the case?"

He shook his head. "No."

"What *did* you talk about?"

He closed his eyes, and for a few moments, I wasn't sure he was going to answer. Eventually, he did. "We talked about dogs mostly. She loves dogs, especially poodles. We talked about the origin of poodles and the fact that they don't shed. We talked about how she does search and rescue with Callie. We talked about some of her previous finds." He paused and looked up as he tried to recall the conversation. "We talked about the fact that I grew up in Tennessee." He colored. "I talked about my dad and a whole lot of other things that had nothing to do with her ex-husband or this case." He shook his head. "It was the elephant in the room, but neither of us brought it up."

We sat and looked at each other for what felt like hours. Harley was a good cop, but he hadn't been at this as long as I had. Technically, he wasn't a detective yet.

He was on loan to Special Crimes to help out. Nevertheless, he knew the rules. He knew what was expected. If we went to court, a good attorney could toss anything we found. He was putting our investigation at risk. As the lead investigator, I had to decide how much of a risk.

ELEVEN

"WHAT ARE YOU going to do?"

I stared at Harley. "You swear there was nothing inappropriate. Nothing that can in any way compromise this investigation?"

Harley held up his left hand and put his right over his heart. "I swear to you there was nothing inappropriate. I did not discuss the case, her ex-husband or our investigation."

He looked contrite, but innocent.

I pointed. "You're out of the search. You are not to be alone with her. You don't call her. You don't talk to her unless I'm present." I stared. "You got it?"

"Got it." He swallowed. "You going to tell Chief Mike?"

Telling Chief Mike that Harley had made a mistake in judgement that could have compromised an open investigation would have ended Harley's time with Special Crimes. There were a lot of eager, young officers who were itching to get the opportunity to help out Special Crimes. It was a leg up toward detective, and Harley knew it. He *was* a good cop. He was smart and had a natural instinct that would serve him well. He was also my friend, but everything took a backseat to the badge, including friendship. It wasn't easy for cops to make friends or find companionship. Most cops were only friends with other cops. It was a lot easier than having a friend tell you something they had done that would force you to arrest them. However, I also remember when I met Paris. She was a suspect in the murder of the choir director at our church. I fell for her, but thankfully, I was quickly able to rule her out as a suspect.

"Look, I'm glad you like Marti. I like her too. Paris likes her, but we have a job to do. I won't tell Chief Mike about this, but you need to promise me that you'll hold off on pursuing things until we can completely rule her out as the murderer."

A weight lifted, and his shoulders raised about two inches. "I promise."

We got up and headed back to the precinct. There was still a charge of electricity between us, and I wasn't sure if things would ever return to the way they'd been. However, for now, we were okay.

Back at the precinct, I took my warrant and enlisted some help with executing my search warrant. Harley stayed behind.

I hated executing that warrant. Marti had been extremely helpful, and I'd worked with her and Callie many times in the past. I knocked and waited for her to open up. When she saw me, her initial response was a smile. However, at seeing the other officers, the blood drained from her face, and she looked as though she would buckle. She didn't.

I handed her the warrant. "I have a warrant to search the premises."

She nodded, took the warrant and then opened the door and stepped back so we could enter.

Callie came up and stood by her human's side. She gave a slight growl, and the officers paused, but Marti reached down and patted her head. "It's okay, girl."

Callie didn't look so sure. She stared at the officers as they entered the house, and her hair stood up. She bared her teeth, but she didn't make a sound.

Marti bent down and put her arms around her dog.

The officers glanced at the dog, but when she didn't move, they entered, split up and got to work.

Marti looked around as though she were looking for someone. "Is that everyone?" she said.

"Yeah. Hopefully, it won't take long, and we'll try not to cause too much disruption."

"What should I do? May I sit down?"

"Yes, if you would just sit over there, we'll get this done as quickly as possible and get out of your hair. If we take anything, we'll give you a receipt, okay?"

Marti and Callie moved to the sofa. Marti sat, and Callie hopped up and sat next to her, keeping her ears attuned to the movement going on in the other rooms.

Executing the warrant hadn't taken long. It was a small house, and she didn't have a lot of stuff. We took her computer, a cell phone, a pair of shoes that were covered with mud and whose tread appeared to match one found at the crime scene. And we took a pair of blue jeans and a jacket that had stains that appeared to be blood.

I handed Marti a receipt for everything we'd taken, and we left. She frowned at the receipt but said nothing.

Back at the precinct, the crime lab took the items to

do what they do. I went to my desk. It would take time for the lab to test the items, and I didn't think they would find much on the laptop they'd taken. However, the stains on the clothes, the shoes and the cell phone would probably yield something.

I had just sat down when Sir Percy stormed up to my desk. "What *exactly* do you think you're doing? There's no bloody way Marti killed anyone."

He needed to blow off steam, so I let him rant about blaming a poor, innocent woman who was a victim, wasting police time and money on a frivolous search. He paced in front of my desk, waving his hands and chomping on an unlit cigar that hung from the side of his mouth. After about a minute or two, rather than winding down, he actually became more enraged. His face was red, and he looked as though he were about to explode. He stopped for breath. His chest heaved as he fumed.

"You done?" I asked.

"No, I'm bloody-well not done, but I might as well be done if this is all the bleeding support I can expect." He marched away and then turned around and marched back. "I quit." He reached in his pocket and pulled out an envelope and slammed it on my desk. Then, he spun around and stomped out.

Harley stared at me but didn't say anything, which was probably worse because his eyes screamed *This is all your fault*.

I pushed around some papers on my desk and stared at my computer screen, although I couldn't recall one thing on it. Eventually, I picked up the paper Sir Percy had left on my desk and gave it a quick read. Then, I shoved my chair back and went down the hall to Chief Mike's office.

The chief glanced up at my knock and waved me in. Before I could speak, he held up a hand. "Sir Percy quit. I heard." He shrugged. "Don't worry about it. He'll get over it."

"How do you know he'll get over it? He's offended that we...that I searched his niece's house." I paced. "He's angry. My partner's angry. My girlfriend will probably be angry when she finds out." I rubbed the back of my neck. "Everyone's angry."

"Percy's upset."

"You think?"

"He gets upset. He quits at least twice a year." He reached down to his desk drawer and pulled out a folder. He plopped it on his desk and opened it. "Sir Percy's letters of resignation."

I stared at the pile. "I had no idea."

"No reason you should. Usually he doesn't resign to a detective. He must really be sore, but he'll get over it. He'll go to the Hair of the Dog and have some drinks. He'll sleep off a hangover tomorrow, and then he'll be back to work as if nothing happened." He took the letter of resignation I had placed on his desk on top of the pile, closed the folder and returned it to his drawer. "Sir Percy quits. I ignore it. He comes back. If he wasn't such a good coroner, I might accept one of his resignations, but he's the best."

I felt my shoulders relax a smidge, but there was a lot of tension in my neck.

Chief Mike gave me a hard stare. "Harley will get over it too. He's young. He's smitten."

I sucked in air.

"You thought I didn't know?" Chief Mike chuck-led. "I know everything that happens in this unit." He leaned back in his chair. "Your girlfriend will get over it too. I got a chance to talk to her at Percy's party. She's a smart cookie. Well, anything else?"

I took that as a dismissal and left.

Harley was waiting for me at my desk. I wasn't in the mood for another round of fighting, but I could tell by his body language that he was excited. "Hey, can I show you something?"

"Sure."

He placed a newspaper article on my desk. The arti-cle was about Bruce Leonard. The reporter accused him of mafia connections, namely Mike Maxwell. When I finished reading, I looked up. "There's not a lot of in-formation here, but everything's circumstantial with few real facts."

Harley placed another article in front of me. This one was an article about the early retirement of a reporter, Howard Banner. When I finished reading, he looked at me like an excited puppy. "Isn't that the old guy you met who lived in that apartment complex across from that lawyer, Richard Stout?"

"Sounds like the same guy, but what do you think he'll be able to tell us? The man is in his mid-eighties."

"Maybe he can tell us if Bruce Leonard was con-nected to Mike Maxwell." When I didn't reply, he said, "Look, you told me to look for other suspects. Bruce Leonard is connected to Maxwell. If Maxwell killed Jake Harrison, then Leonard may be involved."

"You think Mike Maxwell is responsible for Harrison's death?"

"Seems more logical than Marti Alexander. Mike Maxwell is connected. He's dirty, and we know it. We just haven't been able to prove it. You heard what Mayor Longbow said. If we can take Maxwell down, then he's supportive."

"Taking Maxwell down won't be easy."

He grinned. "If it were easy, someone would have done it by now."

I had met Howard Banner when I was investigating the murder of another of St. Joe's elite, JP Rollins. Banner lived in the Tulip Trails apartment complex, which I knew well. I knew it because I used to live there before I bought my townhouse. The complex was nice. There were only four units per building, and none of the units shared walls. That was one of the key selling features in my opinion. There were two apartments on the lower level that were separated by a hallway and two upstairs with a similar layout. The apartments were spacious two-bedroom units with washers and dryers and either a small patio or a balcony, depending on which floor you were on. There were also two garages, one on each end of the building like bookends.

Harley and I drove over to the complex and parked in front of Banner's unit. I rang the intercom and waited. I knew from experience that Howard Banner wasn't the speediest responder. After about a minute, he asked who was there. When I gave my name, I was rewarded by the buzz that unlocked the outer door. The wait for the front door wasn't nearly as long.

"RJ, you're early. I didn't expect you until Sunday.

You can't be in that big of a hurry to get your hind end beat again." He smiled. "Don't tell me I got my days confused."

He stepped aside so Harley and I could enter.

"You don't have your days confused, but your memory is definitely faulty. I'm the one that mopped the floor with you last time."

Howard Banner chuckled. "I don't remember that."

When I had met Mr. Banner, he reminded me a lot of Mama B. He was wise and liked to talk. He also liked to play games; checkers was a favorite. I came by about once every other week, and we talked and played checkers.

He pointed to Harley. "Looks like you brought re-inforcements."

I introduced the two and then continued our trash talking. "I don't need reinforcements to beat you, but I'm here on official police business."

"Well, then you better sit down, unless you've come to arrest me."

Howard Banner was a friendly, elderly gentlemen of eighty-six. His apartment was crammed full of over-stuffed furniture, and nearly every surface was covered with pictures of his wife, who was now deceased, his five brothers, two sisters, six children, fourteen grand-children and fifty-seven great-grandchildren. He liked to talk, and while we played checkers, he had told me about his family and his years of service during World War II, along with the accident that left him with a pur-ple heart and the bullet that he still carried. It was too close to his spine to be removed.

Mr. Banner used a walker to get around. He went

to the dining room table, where the checkerboard was setup. "Can I get you gentlemen anything? Tea or coffee? I'm afraid they won't let me keep anything stronger." He laughed.

We declined, and we all sat down at the dining room table.

"Well, then you better get to your official business."

"I've been coming here a few months, and I don't remember you telling me you were a journalist."

Banner's face changed. The smile left. His brow creased, and for the first time since I've known him, he was angry.

"There's a reason I don't talk about that." His lips formed a straight line, and he looked as though he wanted to spit.

We sat in an uncomfortable silence until Harley decided to break it. "Look, we're investigating a murder. If we can't figure out who the real killer is, then an innocent woman may get arrested. We have reason to believe Bruce Leonard may have been involved and—"

"Bruce Leonard?"

"Yes, he's involved in this somehow, but—"

He stood up and walked out of the room into one of the two bedrooms.

Harley and I exchanged glances. His eyes asked a question, but I didn't know the answer and merely shook my head. We stood up and were about to leave when we heard Howard Banner making his way back to sit down.

Banner had one of those walkers with a basket in front with a leather pad that allowed it to convert into a seat. He had placed a box on the seat and was making his way back into the dining room. Once he returned, he sat down and pointed toward the box. "If you want to know about Bruce Leonard…it's in there."

Harley took the box and placed it on the table. He removed the lid and looked at Mr. Banner, who nodded his approval for us to dig in. And we did.

It took over an hour for us to review and read through all of the articles and notes. Harley and I divided and conquered. We separated the items into piles. The pieces that were useful were all placed in one pile. Some of the documents were merely notes about character, which wouldn't help. In one case, Bruce Leonard had cursed and threatened a process server who had come to serve a warrant. Another document told how Bruce Leonard had decked a man who had tried to repossess his car. Those items we set aside. They indicated Bruce Leonard had a temper and at one time had experienced financial difficulties, but they wouldn't help us prove he'd killed Jake Harrison.

"There's a lot of information here." I glanced over at Howard Banner who was sipping a cup of coffee.

"Thirty-five years I worked for the *St. Joseph Tribune*," Banner said. "I started out writing obituaries and society pieces and worked my way up. I spent twenty years on the cop beat. I made friends with the crime scene guys and with cops. They knew me and respected me." He took a moment to swallow his emotions and then continued. "Well, I started hearing about Bruce Leonard. I heard he was dirty. I heard he was taking bribes, but no one was willing to come forward. They were all too scared. Finally, I got somebody who was willing to talk. They told me Leonard was connected. At first, he was struggling financially, but then after Mike Maxwell moved to St. Joe, suddenly Bruce Leonard was flush. He was wearing expensive clothes and buying fancy cars. He had tons of money then."

Harley flipped through one of the notebooks. "What was he doing to get money from Maxwell?"

"Why do you think every witness the police ever tried to get to testify against Maxwell would *suddenly* go missing, develop amnesia or completely recant their story?" He looked from Harley to me. "Mike Maxwell is a dirty drug-pushing thug, but men like Mike Maxwell don't like getting their hands dirty. They aren't going to do the dirty work themselves. No, they hire buffoons like Bruce Leonard for that."

"You have notes, but I'm not seeing much that would stand up in court," I said.

"That was the problem. I couldn't get anyone who was willing to say anything against him on the record. I thought if I could write the articles, maybe I'd make him mad enough to make a mistake." He pursed his lips. "Apparently, I made him mad alright. But rather than coming after me, he got lawyers to go after the newspaper. They sacked me."

"I'm sorry."

"Thirty-five years and all I got was a lousy pension that barely pays the rent on this apartment." He looked around. "Well, no good deed goes unpunished, right? Leonard made sure I didn't get hired by any other papers. Not that there was a lot of options here in St. Joe, but in the past, I'd had several pieces picked up by the Associated Press, and I had friends in Chicago, but… I was persona non grata." He gave me a hard stare. "You want to know why I don't talk about being a reporter? Well, now you know."

"Do you know why Bruce Leonard left the police force?" I asked. "I remember some kind of investigation by Internal Affairs, but I couldn't find any records of it."

He paused for a while, and I could see the wheels turning as he decided whether we were trustworthy. He must have decided we were. "I was retired by then, but I still had some friends on the force, and they told me that Bruce Leonard was investigated for tampering with evidence."

My heart raced. "Do you remember the details? There's nothing in his file."

Howard Banner let out a long breath. "You're a smart man. What does that tell you?"

I didn't need to think. It was chilling and extremely depressing to think about the implications of what that meant. After a long pause, I asked, "You got any evidence?"

"If you say there's no record you can find, then I think you know there's no evidence. It's been buried."

I collected the articles in the keep pile. "Mind if we take these?"

"If anything in that box will help you nail Bruce Leonard or Mike Maxwell, then you're welcome to it."

TWELVE

BACK AT THE PRECINCT, Harley and I went through the notes and articles we'd collected from Howard Banner again. Apart from the fact that Bruce Leonard may have been connected to Mike Maxwell, there wasn't really anything that would help us with our murder investigation.

"You got anything?" Harley asked.

"Only a crick in my neck." I rubbed the sore spot, stretched and checked the time. "Let's take another look at the crime scene evidence."

We walked back to the evidence room, completed the required paperwork and received a box with everything that had been tagged and bagged from the crime scene. We took the box to a conference room where we could spread everything out. An hour later, we were still going through the gum wrappers and miscellaneous junk.

I held up a bag with an earring. "Interesting that Marti was careless enough to leave one of her earrings at the crime scene, but careful enough to wipe off her fingerprints."

Harley sat up. "I hadn't thought about that."

"It doesn't mean she didn't do it. It just means… I don't know what it means."

"It could mean that someone planted that earring there to try and frame her."

There was such an eagerness in his voice that I didn't have the heart to share the probability of that, so I didn't say anything. Instead, I picked up the bottle of beer I'd noticed at the scene of the crime. "Yuengling...isn't that the beer that President Obama used to drink?"

Harley glanced over my shoulder. "I think so."

I put the bottle back in the box. "This had Jake Harrison's DNA. So, he obviously felt comfortable enough to stand around drinking beer with his killer."

"It doesn't mean that person was Marti."

"I didn't say it was, but maybe we need to find out if Jake Harrison knew Bruce Leonard." Harley looked hopeful, but I glanced at the time. "We'll check him out tomorrow."

He didn't like waiting, but it was getting late, so he relented.

I stopped at a florist and bought a bouquet of Asiatic lilies, which I knew were Paris's favorite, and then I picked up a bottle of wine and drove to her house. We missed going out for date night yesterday, so I was hoping we could catch up today. I rang the bell and waited.

She opened the door, but the look on her face didn't say *Welcome*. In fact, she didn't say anything. She took one look, turned and walked inside. The fact that she left the door open was the only indication I had that I was permitted to enter.

Inside, she was standing in the middle of the living room floor with her arms folded across her chest.

I decided to take the bull by the horns. "I take it you've talked to Marti."

"That poor woman cried. She actually sobbed. RJ, how could you? You know she couldn't possibly have killed that man."

"I don't *know* she didn't. All of the evidence is pointing toward her as the only person with motive, means and opportunity to have killed him, but—"

She waved a hand. "Don't give me that police mumbo jumbo. I'm talking about in your heart, you know she didn't do it." She looked hard in my eyes. "Don't you?"

"Paris, I can't talk about this with you."

"We aren't talking about the case. We're talking about Marti."

"You're splitting hairs. Marti is the center of an investigation. You know I can't talk about an open investigation, even if it's only to discuss my opinion of a suspect."

"Marti is a friend."

Maya came up and sat in front of Paris and glared. Obviously, she knew where her loyalties lie. Something about that dog's accusatory stare pushed me over the top. I put the flowers and the bottle of wine on the coffee table. "I'll let myself out."

I got behind the wheel and drove. I didn't pay attention to where until I found myself on Mama B's alley. I pulled up to her house. She was on the front porch watching a rousing basketball game across the street.

I got out of the car, climbed up onto her porch and kissed her cheek. "Hi, Mama B."

She rocked. "Why didn't you bring the dog?"

"I don't think she's on speaking terms with me at the moment." I flopped into the other rocker on the porch.

For several minutes, we rocked in silence and watched

the basketball game. Mama B broke the silence. "I made some ice cream. Why don't you bring us both a bowl?"

Mama B's ice cream was soft, creamy and delicious. I hopped up and brought us each a bowl. We sat down and ate in peace. When she finished, she said, "What did y'all fight about?"

"What makes you think Paris and I had a fight?"

She smiled and rocked.

Eventually, I found myself baring my soul. I told her about Marti and Harley. I shared Mayor Longbow and Chief Mike's thoughts before getting around to Paris. "Even Maya looked at me like she couldn't believe I had the nerve to arrest the woman who had bred her."

Mama B laughed. "You're just doing your job. Harley knows that. He'll be fine. That boy's in love, and he ain't thinking with his head. Mayor Longbow is just a slick politician. He won't care who you arrest, as long as he can have a press conference that makes him look good." She rocked. "Paris will be fine. She knows you're just doing your job."

"You didn't see the look she gave me."

"I don't need to see it. I know Paris. She's just upset for her friend, but she'll get over it."

I started to object but my cell vibrated. It was Paris. She typed a long apology. Thanked me for the flowers and the wine and invited me to come back where she could apologize in person.

"Based on that smile, I'm guessing she's already over it," Mama B said.

I tried to keep my lips still, but they had a mind of their own and wouldn't stop curving upward. I gave up and let them curve. "She apologized, but…" My head started down another path, which ended the curve. "I can't believe she got upset."

"Pshaw. Y'all just had your first disagreement. You're going to have many more and some of them are going to be over things you consider small, like leaving the seat up on the toilet or not hanging the toilet paper right so it rolls over rather than under, like the Good Lord intended." She looked away, but I could tell she was laughing.

"Wait, what?" I looked at her. "I'm sure God has more important concerns than the way my toilet paper rolls."

"Hmmm… God cares about the things that are important to us. Relationships require give and take. Paris cares about you. Did it ever occur to you that this might be about more than her friend Marti?"

"What do you mean?"

"Women have an instinct about things. We sense things. I think she senses that arresting Marti is a bad move." She rocked. "I think so too."

"You don't even know Marti."

"I don't have to know her. I know you. I know something's bothering you. If you had peace about that woman killing her husband, you would have arrested her and wouldn't need my grandfather's secret recipe so you can get to sleep. I know you're concerned about leaving the police, even though we both know it's time. And I know—"

"Wait, I—"

"Boy, you know better than to interrupt when grown folks is talking."

To my godmother and all of the elderly women at the

church, I would never be *grown*, so I apologized and waited.

She rocked for a few seconds. "Now, I know you've enjoyed being a policeman, and you know I supported you when your mother and father didn't. It was something you had to do, but things change. You've changed. I know it, and you do too. Now, if you stay—" she shrugged "—that's your choice. I will continue to love and support you, but you need to face up to what's been bothering you ever since your accident and deal with it."

Part of me felt angry. Part of me felt relief. I wasn't willing or able to face the relief. So, I couldn't focus at the moment. "I'm not one hundred percent confident that Marti isn't the killer."

"Pshaw."

"All of the evidence is pointing to her. Jake was killed with her gun. There's physical evidence that indicates she was at the park at the time when he was killed. She had a motive."

Mama B rocked.

"Well?"

"Then why haven't you arrested her?"

She had me there. I racked my brain to come up with an answer. "Harley and Paris—"

"Pshaw. You don't bit more care about what Harley and Paris think than the man in the moon. I'm talking about you, Robert James Franklin Junior. If you believed in your heart that woman was a murderer, you would have arrested her." She stopped rocking and stared down her nose at me.

I felt flush. "It's complicated."

She rolled her eyes and started rocking again. "No,

it's not. It's simple. If you saw one of those boys across the street pull out a gun and shoot someone, you would have them in jail so fast it would make their head spin. There's something about this situation that has prevented you from arresting her. Now, you need to face that, and you'll be fine." She handed me her bowl. "Take these bowls in the kitchen. Just leave them in the sink, and I'll wash them later."

I rose, took the bowls and headed into the kitchen.

"There's two containers of ice cream in the deep freezer—one for you and one for Paris. You can take hers over when you go."

I did as I was told. I drove the ice cream to Paris's house and tried not to think about what Mama B said, although no matter how hard I tried to force it down, her comments kept coming back up.

Paris was very sorry and made sure I knew it. I was successfully distracted for a few hours. Unfortunately, when I left, Mama B's words came back to torment me. At home, I thought about taking another round of Mama B's tonic, but I decided to stop avoiding the question. *What was bothering me? Why hadn't I arrested Marti Alexander?*

I went to my garage and started working on the console table Paris wanted. I loved the smell of wood, and using a table saw would force me to concentrate, at least if I wanted to keep all of my digits, which I did. Sanding was another matter entirely. I could use the sander and allow my mind to wander wherever it wanted.

Before the accident, I ran to clear my mind. However, the plate and screws in my knee didn't allow much running anymore. At first, I forced myself. However, it just wasn't worth the pain.

Jake Harrison cheated on his wife and left her for another woman. She was listed as the beneficiary on his insurance policy, according to the General. A million dollars would be considered a motive for murder in anyone's book. We had her shoeprint and earring from the crime scene. We had her cell phone, which had pinged a cell tower near the crime scene at the time of Jake's death. But…something didn't feel right. "Right isn't the proper word," I said aloud to hear myself talk. "Something feels…familiar." Now, why would this crime seem familiar?

Before I could investigate my feeling any further, my cell phone rang. I glanced at the time and realized it was early Friday morning. I felt myself tense. No good messages come at 2 a.m. I pulled out my phone and looked to see who was calling.

My stomach muscles contracted. "Hi, Chris."

"Hey, RJ. I think I left my French book in your car when we went to lunch. I've got a test coming up. Any chance you could bring it? It's got my homework in it."

Before the words left his mouth, I was moving. I ran upstairs and got my keys and my gun. "Absolutely, where are you?"

"I'm at Mr. Maxwell's house. My aunt Marcia got a flat tire, and she wasn't able to pick me up, but Mr. Maxwell offered to bring me home." His voice sounded unnaturally positive and strained. Even if he hadn't used the safe word, I knew he wasn't alone and that he had to be careful what he said. What I didn't know was if someone was listening. I decided to take a chance to find out.

"Well, it's pretty late. Don't you have school tomorrow?"

"Yeah, I suppose it is, plus I have homework to do."

"What's the address?"

I remembered Mike Maxwell's address from the time I'd spent reviewing his file, but I wanted to keep Chris talking.

"Umm, I'm not sure. It's a really big house, and he's got a pool. When the weather is warmer, he said I could come and swim, but I didn't want to swim tonight."

"I'll be there in ten minutes." I backed the car out of the garage. "Why don't you come outside. That will make it easier for me."

I heard him repeating that he needed to go outside for a minute. There was a lot of background noise. Music playing, people talking, and I could barely hear. After a few moments, I heard the wind. "Okay, I'm pulling into his subdivision now."

I rarely had the opportunity to use my concealed LED strobe lights, but I turned them on to allow me to fly through the streets without getting pulled over. When I was a kid and watched old cop shows from the seventies and eighties, I remember thinking how cool those Kojak lights were. Whenever the bald, lollipop eating detective wanted to fly through New York traffic, he would reach in the glove box and pull out his light and put it on the roof of his car and zoom down the streets. Technological advancements meant my lights were installed in my dash and grille. Completely concealed until turned on, they were extremely bright when they were, with the option to strobe and change color.

Mike Maxwell lived in a ritzy neighborhood on the

southside of town. The houses in this subdivision were expensive, and they showed it with columns, oversized custom windows and brick facades. Even if I didn't already know the address, I could have figured out which house belonged to Maxwell. The ornate facade with stone lions guarding the driveway and gold-toned finishes matched Maxwell's personality. Plus, his was the only house in the otherwise quiet subdivision that was lit up and had music blaring. I turned off my lights. When I pulled up in front, Chris was standing on the porch, and he ran and jumped in the car.

"You okay?" I had my gun out and was looking around for Mike Maxwell or any of his security. Men like Maxwell always had security.

Chris buckled his seatbelt. "I'm fine. Can we just go?"

I looked at him. "Seriously, are you?"

He took a deep breath. "I just got scared. Please, can we go?"

His eyes pleaded, so rather than busting into the house and beating Mike Maxwell down or calling vice and having the house raided, I backed out of the driveway and drove away.

We drove for a full five minutes in silence before Chris spoke. "I'm sorry, RJ. I know you said only use the phone and the safe word if I was in trouble, but… I was scared."

"It's okay. I want you to use it, especially if you're scared." I glanced at him out of the corner of my eye. "Do you want to tell me what happened? How did you end up at Mike Maxwell's house at two in the morning?"

He took a deep breath. "I did what you told me. I went

to work. Usually, my aunt Marcia comes around eleven to pick me up, but she didn't come. Then, she called and said she had a flat tire. I was just going to walk home, but she didn't feel comfortable with me walking late at night. Mr. Maxwell was in the office and overheard me. He asked for the phone, and then he told her that he was having a little party at his house. He asked if it would be okay if I went. He said he wanted to thank me for all of my work fixing his computers and that he'd bring me home, but it would be late."

"I can't believe your grandmother was okay with you being out this late on a school night."

"Me either. I mean, normally she'd have a fit if I'm not home by midnight, but Aunt Marcia said she'd clear everything with grandma and it was okay for me to go and stay as long as I wanted." He looked at me. "Can you believe that? The one time I want nothing more than to go home and get in the bed, and she gives me free reign to stay out with a…gangster."

Now that he was safe, and my heart had stopped pounding, I was able to see the humor in his situation, but I forced myself to be serious. "Okay, so your aunt thought she was giving you a treat. You got to go to a party at your wealthy employer's house, I get it. What happened?"

"He drove me to his house, and there were all these people there. I didn't recognize any of them, but they were all dressed up like they were going to a club. He had a DJ and everything. At first, it was okay. I just sat and watched, but then people started getting high."

"You saw them?"

"Yeah, some of them were doing lines and taking pills."

"You didn't take any pills, did you?"

"Nah, but they offered." He reached into his pocket and pulled out a tissue and handed it to me. "I put them in here and just pretended like I was taking them, sort of like I do when grandma tries to make me take vitamins and cod liver oil pills." He scrunched his face.

Since I was driving, I just put the tissue in my pocket until later.

"As the night progressed, these folks were getting lit up! They were drinking and snorting and taking pills, and then they started taking off their clothes and jumping in the pool." He shook his head. "All I could think was if my grandmother caught me here, she would tan my hide and then I'd be grounded until I was old enough to get social security. And I'm not kidding. Man, she would have been furious if she thought I was around anybody doing drugs. So, I called you."

"I'm glad you did." I asked a few other questions, but it didn't seem that Chris was in any danger, which helped to slow my heart rate down. I pulled in front of Sister Green's house and wasn't surprised to see the lights on.

Chris glanced up. "I sure hope Aunt Marcia remembered to call, or I'm going to need protecting from her."

"You want me to go in with you?"

"Nah, I think I better take this one alone." He reached in the backseat and grabbed his backpack. He opened the car door. "Thanks for coming, RJ."

"You're welcome. Hang onto that phone, okay?"

He got out and slammed the door. "You bet. It's nice to have Five-O on speed dial."

I waited to make sure he got in safely, and then I pulled away.

When I got home, I wasn't in the mood for wood-working, so I went upstairs and made a cup of coffee. I was going to need to start getting ready for work in a few hours anyway.

I sat at my barstool and pulled out the tissue and took a look. There were several small pink pills with what appeared to be an S, like the Superman logo, on them. I would need the lab to analyze the pills to be sure, but I was pretty confident they were Ecstasy. Part of me wanted to call the drug squad. A raid wouldn't look good with Mister-I-Am-A-Law-Abiding-Citizen's record. However, I didn't want Maxwell to hold any-thing against Chris. I wouldn't want him to realize how important Chris was to me because if things went bad between us, and I felt sure they would, I didn't want him hurting Chris to get to me. Besides, he would just deny any knowledge of drugs. Chris wouldn't testify. So, there was nothing to tie him to anything.

This case was getting more and more confusing, and no matter how hard I tried, I struggled to get Mama B's words out of my head. So, rather than fighting against them, I opened myself up to them. Was she right? Was there truth there?

When it came to Marti Alexander, I played back what I knew about her. My gut told me she didn't do it. My gut wouldn't hold up in court, but all of my instincts told me that she wasn't the murderer. In spite of the evidence, it just didn't fit. It didn't feel right. Feelings and gut instinct may not be much but trusting them had kept me alive over the years, and I had learned to rely on them. I decided to rely on them again. That was enough internal soul searching for one day. I decided to push everything else Mama B said to the back of my mind and focus on the case. If Marti Alexander didn't murder her husband, who did?

Green trees are bending
Po' sinner stand a-trembling
The trumpet sounds within-a my soul
I ain't got long to stay here

THIRTEEN

It DIDN'T TAKE long to shower and dress, and I was at the precinct early. I dropped the pills Chris got from the party at the lab. The lab tech looked at the pills and declared them Ecstasy, but he'd run the tests just to confirm.

I went back through my notes and the evidence, and by the time Harley arrived, I was ready to tackle someone who I felt merited a closer look.

We found the address for Bruce Leonard and headed out.

Based on the information Howard Banner had collected, I had a feeling Bruce Leonard would live what Mama B called "high on the hog." I wasn't disappointed. He lived in a condo that overlooked the St. Thomas River. I lived near the St. Thomas River too, but my townhouse wasn't in the heart of downtown.

We entered the glass and steel building and were greeted by a concierge. When asked how he could help, we flashed our shields and asked for directions to Bruce Leonard's apartment. When he picked up the phone to call, I mentioned we'd prefer not to have our presence announced and were directed toward the elevator.

We took the elevator to the top floor. There were only two units. We knocked.

After a few minutes, Bruce Leonard opened the door. "Can I help you?"

Again, we showed our shields.

Leonard opened his door and stepped back for Harley and me to enter. Once we were inside, he closed the door. "What brings two of St. Joseph's finest to my door?"

Bruce Leonard was in his mid-thirties, five foot ten and two hundred pounds. He worked out, and it showed. He had short dark hair, dark eyes and a cocky smile, which I wanted to wipe off his smug face.

"We're investigating the murder of Jake Harrison."

"Never heard of him."

"We couldn't help but notice your car at his house earlier this week. It's a black 1969 Chevy Camaro Z28/SS coupe, right? Two white stripes. It's hard to miss a car like that."

I noticed the muscle in his jaw twitch. If I hadn't been looking, I wouldn't have seen it. He had a good poker face.

"You must know a lot about cars."

"I love cars, but a beauty like that '69 Camaro is hard to miss."

He relaxed a bit. "Forgive my manners. Would you gentlemen like something to drink?"

We declined.

"I hope you don't mind if I get myself something."

The living room, dining room and kitchen were one big open space. He walked over to the sleek stainless steel and black modern kitchen and got a beer from the fridge. He twisted off the top and took a swig. "Please, have a seat."

I wondered if he could find other ways to stall, but he must have realized we knew it was his car or we wouldn't be here.

"Now, you were asking about my car?"

"Actually, I was asking about your relationship with Jake Harrison."

"I didn't have a relationship with Jake Harrison."

After a manly five-second stare down, he smiled. "My relationship was with Mrs. Harrison. I went to give my condolences. That's all."

"Do you know Mrs. Harrison well?"

"Fairly well, yes."

"Where were you last Saturday evening?"

He took another drink and smiled. "Am I a suspect?"

"We like to be thorough when we're investigating a case. No loose ends." I chuckled. "You remember how that is. You were a cop once."

His grip tightened on his beer. The vein in his jaw pulsed again, and his eyes looked almost black. He was seething. "I don't know...let me think..." He paused and looked to the ceiling as he struggled to remember. "I think I was home alone." He smiled. "Too bad I didn't know I'd need an alibi."

As a former cop, he knew most innocent people didn't have an alibi. Murderers have watched enough television to know they'll need one.

Harley glanced around the high-rise condo. "This is one nice place. You must be doing pretty well now that you've retired from the police department. What do you do?"

The condo was a modern bachelor pad. The floors were polished concrete, and the space had a two-story living room with one wall that was covered with floor-to-ceiling glass windows that overlooked the river. The color scheme was black and gray and lacked warmth and personalization, but I didn't have to live there, so it was fine.

He leaned against the counter with his arms folded. "I do a little bit of this and little bit of that. I managed my money well and made good investments."

I wanted to smack the smug look off his face. "Word on the street is that you're working for Mike Maxwell."

His eyes were stone cold, and for an instant, I got a glimpse into his soul. I felt a shiver run down my spine, and my hand made an involuntary move toward my gun.

"Do I make you nervous, Detective Franklin?"

"Not in the least." I forced myself to smile, but I suspected it looked more like a grimace. "I think I would like that drink, though. If you don't mind."

He narrowed his eyes but smiled and opened the fridge. He got another beer and handed it to me.

I twisted the top off and took a sip.

We all stared at each other.

"Tell me about your car?" I said. "When did you get it?"

His face lit up, and we talked cars for a few minutes. He was knowledgeable, and as we talked, I could see his shoulders relax.

Once his body language changed, I asked, "How did you meet Carolyn Harrison?"

The shift was instant, and he was back on high alert.

His jaw muscle tensed, and his right eye twitched. "Beats me."

I knew we weren't going to get anything from him. He was too slick for that.

He reached out a hand. "You finished with that?"

"No worries. I'll finish it in the elevator and toss it downstairs."

Bruce Leonard gave me a hard stare, but he must have decided I was wasting my time because he gave me a smile and shrugged. He picked up his own bottle and took a sip.

I reached out a hand. "I can take your bottle if you want."

He laughed. "No, thanks. My bottle and my DNA will stay right here unless you have a court order demanding it."

Harley and I took the elevator to the bottom floor. Once we were outside, I poured the remaining beer out before getting in the car.

"What was all that about the beer?" Harley asked.

"This is the same brand that we found at the crime scene."

His face lit up for a moment, but the excitement quickly faded. "Great, but how will that help us? Lots of people drink beer. Unless you're planning to get his DNA. As of right now, all we have is yours."

"We don't have enough to take to the district attorney to get his DNA, but I remembered something I saw when I was watching television with Mama B last night."

He smiled. "What did The Oracle have to say?"

Harley always referred to Mama B as The Oracle. He

joked that she was a combination of the Oracle of Delphi and the Oracle from *The Matrix* movies.

"She said Marti didn't kill her husband."

"I agree, but…" Harley frowned. "Has she ever met her? Or was this some sixth sense kicking in?"

"Neither. She said she didn't need to know Marti because she knew me. According to her, if I thought Marti was guilty, I would have arrested her by now."

He paused. "She's probably right."

"Yeah, I know."

Back at the precinct, we tested my theory. We went back to the Evidence Room and took out the beer bottle. It was the same brand, but more importantly, it had the same numbers on it. I looked up the number for Yuengling Brewery and asked for the manager. It took several transfers before I got someone who understood what I was looking for and could tell me the information I needed. His name was George. He was one of the plant managers, and he was able to explain what numbers on a bottle of beer are and what they meant. According to George, the numbers were the production code.

He had the raspy voice of a long-time smoker, but he spoke with confidence and excitement. He knew his stuff. "For Yuengling, the production code is an eleven-digit number located on the bottom of the can or on the neck of the bottle. You say you have a bottle?"

"Yeah."

"The production code includes the Julian dates."

I put the phone on speaker and scrambled to get a pen. "Wait. This is a lot of information. What's a Julian date?"

Harley handed me a notepad, and I furiously took notes.

He chuckled. "You want the long or the short version?"

"Let's start with the short version. Although, if this case goes to court, you may have to explain the long version."

He sobered up at the reminder that this was a serious matter. "The short version is that the Julian date refers to a calendar proposed by Julius Caesar in 46 BCE. It's mostly used by astronauts. It's basically a continuous count of the number of days." He babbled on about an epoch and universal time and a lot of other mumbo jumbo that meant nothing to me.

I glanced at Harley, who had the same dazed look in his eyes that I felt must have been in mine. "If that's the short version, then I'm afraid to ask about the long one."

He took a deep breath. "It's a number that will allow us to figure out the exact day and time that a beer was bottled."

"Okay, that makes sense."

"If you look at the bottle. There should be eleven digits. The first two digits are the year it was produced."

Harley held up the bottle. We found the two numbers, and I wrote down the current year. "Okay, got it."

"The next three digits are the day of the year in the Julian Calendar. It might be easier if you just read those off, and I can tell you what they are."

"Zero. Three. Two."

"Okay, so that's zero thirty-two. That's February first. The thirty-second day of the year."

I wrote down the month and day. "Okay. Got it."

"The next digit will tell you where it was produced. We have three breweries. Two of them are in Pottsville,

Pennsylvania. If it's a one, that's our original historic location on the hillside of Mahantongo Street, and it's been in operation since 1831. We produce beer, but it's mostly used for tourists. In early 2001, we opened our state-of-the-art Mill Creek location on the other side of town in Pottsville. If the number is a three, then the beer was manufactured at Mill Creek. If it's a two, then it came from our brewery in Tampa, Florida."

"It's a three."

"That's Mill Creek."

I wrote down *Mill Creek*. "Great. Now what?"

"The seventh digit is the production line number, and the last four digits show the military time it was produced."

I looked at the bottle and wrote. *Production Line one and 11:08.*

Harley and I compared the bottle from evidence with the bottle I took from Bruce Leonard's home. The numbers were exactly the same.

"Okay, so I have two bottles that have the exact same numbers," I said. "What does that tell you?"

George chuckled. "It tells me those two bottles came from the same package."

"Why?"

"The production number can identify beer down to fifteen-minute increments. The probability that you could have two bottles of beer with the exact same numbers that came from different cases is over a million to one."

"You're sure?"

"Conservatively, we're talking one million to one. It's probably a lot higher odds."

"George, you may be called upon to testify in court."

"Well, alright. I never been in a court before."

"We're going to send an officer to take an official statement from you." I took down his name, address and telephone number and told him someone from the local police would be in touch.

When I hung up, Harley wanted to go immediately and arrest Bruce Leonard.

"On what charge? Drinking with someone who was killed?"

His face fell. "But we know the beer Jake Harrison drank came from the same case as the beer in his refrigerator? He had to have been at the scene of the crime or how did his beer get there?"

"Hold your horses. I agree, but we have to have more than beer bottles to prove he murdered Jake Harrison or was even involved in the murder. If we show up with two bottles of beer, his lawyer will just say he gave a couple bottles to Carolyn, who took them to Marti's house, and then Marti took them with her when she went to meet Jake and murder him. We need a motive."

"Carolyn Harrison. Maybe he was having an affair with Jake's wife and wanted to remove all obstacles between him and Carolyn."

"If he's having an affair with her, then it doesn't look as though there were any obstacles between them. We need more, but I agree the key will be his relationship with Carolyn Harrison."

"I can't see Carolyn Harrison murdering her husband. She might break a nail."

I smiled. "She may be a lot tougher than she looks. In fact, if she's been hanging out with Bruce Leonard, then I'm sure she is."

"We can't just go up to her and ask her if she's having an affair with Bruce Leonard."

"That's where you're wrong. We're the police, and we're investigating a murder. We have the right to ask all sorts of questions." I leaned back in my chair. "Of course, she has the right to refuse to answer, but we can ask. I'm just not sure if we want to show our hand yet."

"What's our hand?"

I came to a decision and grabbed my jacket and stood up. "Let's go. I think I know someone who might be able to give us some answers."

FOURTEEN

I DIDN'T EXPECT The General to be at home. In fact, I was counting on him not being there. When Harley and I went to the door, Sister Young answered.

"RJ, I wasn't expecting you. The General isn't here."

"I'm not here to see him. I need to talk to you."

She stared at me a moment but then opened the door wide for us to enter. "I was just getting ready to make myself a cup of tea and take a break. Come on back to the kitchen." She closed the door and turned to lead the way, but she stopped after a few steps. "And wipe your feet. I just finished mopping this entire floor, and I don't intend to to start over."

Harley and I went back and wiped our feet before following her through the house to the kitchen.

The General's house was big, but it wasn't built for families that spent time sitting at the kitchen table. This kitchen, which was closed off at the back of the house, was small and intended for the maid's use rather than the woman of the house. Nevertheless, the room was warm and welcoming. There were terra cotta tiles on the floor, and the walls were yellow with white cabinets. There was a small table near the back window and just enough chairs for the three of us. Harley and I sat, while Sister Young got two more coffee mugs from the cabinet. She placed a tea tin on the table and filled the mugs with hot water from the tea kettle that had just started to whistle. She put the mugs on a tray along with sugar and cream and brought it to the table. She distributed the mugs and sat.

We put a tea bag in our mugs and waited for them to seep. Harley wasn't a fan of tea and added sugar and cream to his mug. Sister Young and I drank our tea black. We sat and enjoyed our tea in silence for several moments.

When she had drank half her cup. She put down her mug and looked at me. "Okay, what did you want to talk to me about?"

"I wanted to talk to you about Jake's wife, Carolyn." I watched her face and wasn't surprised when she scrunched her nose as though she'd just smelled sour milk. "What can you tell me about her?"

"What's to tell. She's a homewrecking tramp. She seduced poor Jake." She frowned. "I know it takes two to tangle, but that one's slick. She knew exactly what she was doing." She glanced out of the window for a moment. "When she first started working for him, she used to call all the time. Then, he started working later and later." She pursed her lips and shook her head. "Poor Mrs. Marti used to worry herself sick about him. She thought he was out drinking or gambling or… God only knows what, but I knew. She used to call here and ask if I'd seen him. I hated telling her that I hadn't. Anyway, she found out about them and was mad enough to spit nails, and I don't blame her." She turned in her seat and stared at me. "Can you believe she actually found them together in her own bed?"

Harley nearly choked on his tea. "You mean in the same house where he was living with his wife?"

"In the same bed! Looks like he could have taken that floozy to a motel."

Sister Young was actually not helping Marti's cause. If Marti found them together in her own bed, then she might have been angry enough to murder both of them. "So, what happened? Did she put them out?"

"Nah. She was proud. They lived in a small house when they first got married. However, when The General saw them doing well, he bought them that big house as a gift. Marti never liked that big house no way. She moved out." She sipped her tea. "You can bet I wouldn't have moved out. I would have put him out, but she said she didn't want anything to do with the house or Jake." She shook her head. "She just took her dog and moved into that little house on the Eastside of town. She got a divorce and wouldn't take alimony either." She nodded toward me. "That just shows you what kind of woman she is." She nodded a few more times. "Class. That's what Miss Marti is, not like that tarted up harlot."

"So, Marti and Jake divorced, and he married Carolyn?" I asked.

"She wasn't about to let him get away, although I don't think Jake wanted to marry her. I think he'd cooled off a lot after everything hit the fan. I will always believe he loved Miss Marti and would have gone back to her if she'd have taken him back...and if that woman would have left him alone long enough to let him think. The day after his divorce was final, she drug him down to the justice of the peace and they were married." She glanced down her nose at me. "That shows you what type of woman she is too. I mean, she didn't even wait a decent amount of time. Oh, she wasn't going to take a chance that he might come to his senses and dump her. She wasn't going to risk losing her meal ticket."

"My understanding is she doesn't get anything."

She gave me a *you poor pitiful thing* look. "Women like that will always find a way to get money. She's probably started hocking everything in that house and will have it on the market before Jake is laid to rest. You mark my words, she has a policy on him, just as sure as my name's Mattie Young."

"What about other men? Do you think she's…ah, seeing anyone else?"

"Lord a mercy. Of course, she is. A woman like that ain't gonna ever be without a man."

"Have you ever seen her with someone? Or heard her mention anyone specific?" I didn't want to mention Bruce Leonard because she was already biased against Carolyn Harrison. Knowingly or unknowingly, if I gave her a name, she might swear that she heard Jake mention him. I would feel better if she volunteered a name.

She thought for a few moments, but then she shook her head. "Like I said, a woman like that ain't gonna be without a man, but she ain't never mentioned anybody to me. Nah, the only other man I've ever heard her mention was some personal trainer." She pursed her lips and gave me a knowing glance. "Her and Jake used to argue about him. Now, what was his name?" She tapped her fingers on the table.

Harley and I waited anxiously.

"I know, it was Bruce… I don't know his last name. She just called him Bruce, but I don't think Jake liked him much. There was something about him… I don't know what it was, but I think Jake was scared of him." She shrugged. "Anyway, that's the only man I ever heard her talk about."

We thanked her for the tea and left.

We decided to make another trip to Carolyn Harrison's. This time there was no muscle car in her driveway, but that didn't mean she was alone. The house had three attached garage bays, and he might have parked in one of them, deciding it was better to avoid attention. Regardless, we rang the bell and were greeted by the same surly housekeeper.

"We'd like to see Mrs. Harrison."

"She's not here."

I pushed the door open. "That's okay, we'll wait."

"Do you have a warrant?"

"Mrs. Harrison isn't under arrest, and we aren't here to search the house. We just want to talk to her, but we can get a warrant if needed."

"That won't be necessary." Carolyn Harrison came around the corner. "How can I help you, Detectives?"

The housekeeper pursed her lips, turned and walked away.

"We have a couple more questions we'd like to ask you." I looked toward the living room. "Maybe we could sit down?"

She stood with her arms crossed for about five seconds, but then she huffed and marched into the living room and flopped down on the sofa.

Harley and I followed. We weren't invited to sit, but we sat anyway.

"First, we just need to confirm your statement that you were with Marti Alexander when your husband was murdered," I said. "You were together all night on Friday and then Saturday morning?"

She examined her nails as though evaluating her last manicure. "That's what I said."

"Do you know anyone who would want to harm your husband?" I made sure my face remained neutral, but I watched her like a hawk.

She unfolded her arms. "No, Jake was harmless."

Harley cleared his throat. "But he was violent. You said he hit you."

She flushed. "Well, he was harmless when he wasn't drinking."

"But when he had been drinking, then he was violent?"

She flicked her hair back. "He could be, yes."

"Can you think of anyone who benefits financially from your husband's death?" I asked.

"Well, now that you mention it…" She leaned forward. "His ex-wife benefits."

"How is that?" I asked. "I mean, you're his wife. Why wouldn't you benefit?"

She took a deep breath. "I should benefit, but his family never liked me, especially his grandfather… The General always looked down on me, like I wasn't good enough for Jake." She rolled her eyes. "All of the provisions for Jake in his trust listed Marti as beneficiary, not me. So, if anyone benefitted from Jake's death, it was Marti. She was the beneficiary for the trust, and

I believe they had an insurance policy together when they got married."

"Do you know how much the insurance policy was for?"

She paused and gazed up as though she had to remember, but I could tell she already knew the answer. "I believe it was a million dollars."

Harley whistled. "That's a lot of money."

She waved a hand. "It's nothing compared to how much The General has." She looked around. "That should have come to me. I'm his wife, not Marti."

Harley turned up his southern charm and accent. "Will you be able to make it without your husband?"

"Well... I'll be okay for a short while. I have a little money of my own, but—" she glanced around "—I'll have to sell the house and move into something smaller. I certainly won't be able to make the mortgage payment on this place by myself."

"I'm sorry to hear that, but Jake wouldn't leave you completely destitute, would he?" I said. "Surely, he took out another insurance policy...something that would allow you to be able to maintain your standard of living. Usually, when a man gets married, he takes care of things like that. Have you checked his papers? There might be another policy. Would you like us to take a look for you? I'd hate to see you lose your house. That would be horrible."

Carolyn Harrison snapped her fingers. "Now that you mention it, I do remember Jake saying he was going to get another insurance policy to make sure I was taken care of."

Harley stood. "That's great. We can take a look and help you get in contact with the company."

"No...ah, thank you, but that won't be necessary. Jake's papers are a real mess, and it would take hours to sift through everything. I'll take care of it." She smiled. "But thank you both for thinking of it. I might never have thought about it if you hadn't triggered that memory." She stood up and turned to escort us out.

"Great. Well, if you would like some help going through those papers, please be sure to let us know. We'll be more than happy to help."

"Mrs. Harrison," I said, "are you familiar with a man named Bruce Leonard?"

She stopped and turned back around. "Bruce Leonard? Why, yes...he's my personal trainer. Why do you ask?"

"Was Bruce Leonard also your husband's trainer?"

"No... Jake wasn't into physical fitness. Of course, I tried to encourage him to join me and get in shape, but...well, Jake just wouldn't come."

"Was that because your husband didn't like Bruce Leonard?"

"No...no. Of course, not. I don't think Jake ever met Bruce...ah, Mr. Leonard."

"We heard that Jake had objections to Bruce Leonard. If the two of them never met, can you tell us what, specifically, your husband objected to?"

Her eyes widened. "I don't know what...who told you Jake objected?"

"We can't divulge our sources, but your husband was overheard."

She narrowed her eyes and her chest heaved. "It was that housekeeper... Mrs. Young. She hates me and was always taking Jake's side. She must have been the one who told you. Well, she's wrong. Jake never *objected* to Bruce, but Jake was jealous. He didn't like the idea of any man helping me workout, that's all."

We waited. When the silence grew too much, she filled it. "Bruce is my personal trainer. There was never anything going on with us…well, not at first. However, Bruce and I have grown very close and…about a month ago, our relationship developed into more." She leaned forward and batted her eyelashes at me. "I know people will think that I never really cared for Jake and that I only married him for his money, but they'd be wrong. You can see that, can't you?"

There it was. She and Bruce Leonard were involved. If she thinks we're stupid enough to believe there was nothing going on before, then all the better.

"Mrs. Harrison, we are not the morality police. What you do in your personal life is your business. We are merely here to investigate the murder of your husband. However, it's always better if you tell us everything up-front rather than wait until we uncover things during the course of the investigation."

"Oh yes, of course. I see that now. It's just… I guess it's silly, but I didn't want you to think poorly of me."

"Please, don't worry about that."

She had admitted that she and Bruce Leonard were having an affair. That was what we needed to know. I glanced at Harley, and we stood up to go. We walked toward the door, but this time she halted us.

"Detectives, I've been thinking about the question you asked earlier…was I with Marti Alexander all night.

Well, now that you know the truth about me and Bruce, I might as well tell you everything. I left the house."

Harley pulled out his notepad again. I could tell by the set of his chin that he wasn't happy.

"What time did you leave?" I said.

She pondered. "I had to wait until Marti went to sleep...or at least I thought she was asleep. I think it was around twelve. Then, Bruce met me outside, and I got in the car with him. We went to his place and...you know." She lowered her eyes.

"Did anyone see you?"

"I'm sure the doorman at his building must have seen us."

"How long were you there?"

She giggled. "We were together all night. Although, I got up early to make sure I was back at Marti's before she woke up." She gazed into the distance. "I'd say I got back around four."

"Was Marti there?"

She gave me a wide-eyed stare. "I don't know. I assumed that she was, but I didn't go into her room to check. I mean, she must have been. Where could she have gone?"

Where indeed.

FIFTEEN

IN ONE FELL SWOOP, Carolyn Harrison had not only given herself an alibi, stating she had been with Bruce Leonard, she also eliminated Marti's.

Harley unleashed a furious tirade against Carolyn Harrison, Bruce Leonard and the decay of the institution of marriage in the twenty-first century. "My grandparents were married for over fifty years, and my parents have been married for thirty. What's wrong with people today?"

I wouldn't have answered that question even if I had an answer to give. Instead, I allowed him to rant while I drove.

Back at the precinct, I had my new plan. "Harley, I want you to find out what insurance company Jake Harrison used. You should start with The General or his dad. They might know. Or maybe you can call Marti."

He squinted at me. "Is this a trap? You didn't want me to have anything to do with her."

I smiled. "Not a trap. Just utilizing my resources. She knows you. She likes you. She probably trusts you more than she does me right now. I just want you to call her. I'm not sending you out on a date."

He gave me a long look, not sure if he was being set up.

I laughed. "I can call her if you don't think you can handle it. I just thought maybe you'd want to."

His glance softened, and he relaxed his shoulders. "Thanks."

I needed to clear my head and sift through everything. So, I grabbed my keys and headed out. I drove to MACU. I parked in the staff lot. Since it was fall break, the lot was mostly empty. The campus had two lakes, and I started walking around them.

Marti Alexander's goose was cooked. Her alibi was gone. Carolyn Harrison may have been guilty of adultery, but she and Bruce Leonard could alibi each other. I made a mental note to confirm with the doorman. Marti could have left the house and killed Jake and returned before Carolyn returned. Marti's gun was the murder weapon. Plus, she stood to gain from the trust The General had established. She was also the likely beneficiary of a million-dollar insurance policy. No matter how I looked at it, things did not look good for Marti Alexander.

So, why didn't I believe that Marti Alexander was the murderer? While I walked, I tried to figure out what was bothering me. In addition to the two lakes, there was a large reflecting pool in front of the library. In the spring, the pool was full of ducks and ducklings. There were quite a few of the inhabitants who had yet to travel south since the weather was nice. I sat on a bench and watched the ducks. That's when I remembered what Mama B had said: "If it walks like a duck and talks like a duck, then it's probably a duck." My gut told me

Marti Alexander wasn't a murderer. She didn't act like a murderer. However, Bruce Leonard was a different breed altogether. I could easily see him killing someone, especially if that person stood between him and something he wanted. Everything associated with the murder fit Bruce Leonard's personality. While I didn't know much about Carolyn Harrison, there was something about her that made me suspicious. But how did they do it?

That's when the tumblers started to click. My brain started playing "What if." What if Carolyn Harrison had drugged Marti? She could easily have slipped something into her drink to ensure that Marti would sleep for a long time. That would explain why Marti was so groggy when I saw her on Saturday morning. I pulled out a notepad and made a note to check with Sir Percy. It was almost a week later, but depending on what was used to drug her, there might be a chance there was still some of it in her system. I put the notepad down. We didn't have time for notes. I pulled out my cell and dialed Harley. When he picked up, I started at once.

"Look, I need you to go and pick up Marti Alexander and—"

"I thought you didn't believe she was guilty—"

"You're wasting time. Listen, I've been thinking maybe she was drugged. If so, it may be too late. It may not be in her system anymore, but we need to try. Pick her up and…you better take Sir Percy with you. He'll know what tests to tell the hospital to run."

"Hospital? Can't Sir Percy—"

"No, he can't. He's related to her…well, sort of related. He's not impartial and a good lawyer would toss out everything. He can go with you to the hospital and talk to the doctors, but he can't be connected with the evidence."

I could tell by his breathing he was moving. "Okay, I'm headed to Sir Percy's office now."

I remembered Chief Mike's words. "He won't be there. Try the Hair of the Dog Pub. If he's not there, try his house."

"Hair of the…never mind. I'm on it." He hung up.

For the first time all week, I felt like things were moving. We were doing something. Even though the odds were slim, it felt good. I had an idea of how the murder was done, but I would need a lot more evidence before I could prove it.

SIXTEEN

I HURRIED BACK to my car so I could get to the precinct. I realized that I was looking at this murder all wrong.

Back at the precinct, I went to the lab and talked to one of the people who worked on trace evidence. St. Joe wasn't a large metropolis, so we didn't have nearly the resources of large cities. However, we did have a great team of men and one woman who worked on trace evidence. I had a quick conversation with one of the people and told them what I was looking for.

Then, I reviewed all of the statements again. After a couple of hours, my cell phone rang. One glance told me it was Harley.

I didn't finish saying *Hello* before he started. "You were right. They used Diazepam or Valium."

"That was quick."

"I might have told them it was crucial for a murder investigation."

"Did they say how long it's been in her system?"

"They can't really tell, but it could be as long as ten days. We were lucky they chose that drug. Not all drugs stay in the system that long. That's probably why she's been complaining about having a headache."

"Great. Is Sir Percy with you?"

"Yeah, we picked him up at the pub on our way to the hospital."

"Good. Ask Marti to make a list of everything she ate and drank on Friday night—and I mean everything. Then take her home. I'm sending a team to the house to collect everything on her list from the house so we can test it."

"Gotcha. We should be there in thirty minutes."

We hung up and for the first time since this case started, I felt the exhilaration that comes when you figure out whodunit and you know how to prove it.

When Harley returned, I had gotten the new report from the trace evidence team and had just started reviewing it.

Harley glanced over my shoulder. "What you got?"

I explained that I asked the trace team to go over several of the items from the crime scene again.

"I don't understand what you were looking for. Those guys are usually really thorough."

"When they did their initial report, they didn't have anyone to compare some of their evidence against. We took Marti's shoes from her house. We know they're Marti's. They checked the mud on the bottom of the shoes to make sure it was consistent with the mud at the crime scene. They also checked the shoe tread pattern compared to one at the crime scene and got a match. What they didn't check was the DNA inside the shoes. They're Marti's shoes, so no need to verify they're her shoes." I leaned back and waited.

"Okay, so what?"

"Since they knew they were her shoes, they didn't check to see if it was her DNA inside the shoes."

"Wait, what do you mean?"

"I mean, could someone else have been wearing the shoes?" I held up the report. "And it looks like I was right. They found skin cells inside the shoes. Some of them belonged to Marti, but some of them belonged to Carolyn Harrison."

"Wait, how did you get Carolyn Harrison's DNA to check? Does she have a record?"

"Nope. Remember that scarf she gave me…well, I gave it to them, and they were able to compare the skin cells they found inside Marti's shoes to the skin cells found on the scarf, and guess what?"

He grinned. "It was a match?"

I nodded. "So, we know Carolyn Harrison wore Marti's shoes. I can't imagine those two were so close that they made a habit of sharing clothing."

Harley sat down. "Walk me through it."

"I think Carolyn Harrison showed up at Marti's door on Friday night, claiming Jake had beaten her."

"Did he?"

I shrugged. "Who knows? Someone sure did, but Marti said he didn't have a history of violence. The only person who ever claimed he got violent enough to actually hit her was Carolyn."

"Okay, so she goes to Marti's house."

"Which was always weird. I mean, she had an affair with Marti's husband and ruined their marriage. Now, when she needed a place to hide, she chooses Marti's house? Why not go to Bruce Leonard's? If Jake came looking for her, surely she could count on Bruce to protect her."

"True."

"She and Leonard go to the house and slip Valium in her food or drink. Marti goes to sleep, and that's when Carolyn *and* Bruce go to work."

"They were in it together?"

"Had to be. They grab her shoes and cell phone and one of her earrings. They use Marti's phone to call Jake and get him to meet them at the river. They probably even took her car. She was drugged and wasn't going anywhere. It wouldn't have been hard to grab her keys from her purse. We should probably have the team check for Carolyn's and Bruce's DNA in Marti's car. Anyway, they drive to the river and wait until Jake shows up." I paused. "I don't think Bruce would have been around. He would have made himself scarce, but he brings some beer with him. Carolyn gets out, and she and Jake drink their beers. Jake would be at ease. He's with his wife. He's drinking beer. That's when one of them, Carolyn or Bruce, pull out Marti's gun that they took from the house and shoot him. Carolyn makes sure to get mud on the shoes, and she drops Marti's earring."

Harley stared at me. "Wow. That sounds pretty complicated. Why?"

"Carolyn is a gold digger. She sets her sights on Jake Harrison, never mind that he's already married. She's an attractive woman, and Jake is weak. They have an affair, and Marti divorces Jake. Now, Carolyn convinces him to marry her, thinking she'll be rich. However, no one likes her. The General refuses to acknowledge that she's his wife and won't change the trust. They won't even bother to make her the beneficiary on his life insurance." I looked at Harley. "By the way, did you have any luck with the insurance companies?"

"I almost forgot." He reached over to his desk, picked up a paper and handed it to me. "I found out she got a million-dollar insurance policy on Jake Harrison. I doubt if he even knew she did it."

"Can you do that? I would think you would need the person's consent to take out an insurance policy. Otherwise, people could just take out insurance policies on anyone they wanted and then bump them off so they can collect."

"I called the insurance company and learned that you can take out insurance as long as you have an insurable interest." He paused and flipped through his notebook. "Basically, it means the person has to have a good reason. If something happened to the person, the other person would be harmed without the policy. A wife would have a good reason to insure her husband. If something happened to Jake, Carolyn loses her income."

"Makes sense. I guess that's why business partners will sometimes have insurance policies on each other. If something happened to one partner, then the business could suffer."

"Exactly."

"Of course, she may have just forged his signature too."

"No one would have contested it." Harley looked at me. "You know what this means? We have the M.O.M."

"Carolyn Harrison was having an affair with Bruce Leonard, and she wanted out of her marriage. She had the means to kill her husband, and she had one million reasons to commit murder, which is one heck of a motive."

SEVENTEEN

WHILE WE WERE TALKING, Chief Mike stuck his head out of his office and yelled my name.

"I've been summoned, but you keep working. Swing by Bruce Leonard's and verify with the concierge that Carolyn Harrison and Bruce Leonard were both there Friday night." I headed for the chief's office but stopped halfway and turned back to Harley. "Don't forget to take a picture. You should have the ones you took of her bruises on your cell."

He nodded and headed out.

By the time I got to Chief Mike's office, I saw that this wasn't going to be a one-on-one meeting. Inside the office was Detective Jennifer Rodriguez. Detective Rodriguez was tall, thin and hard as nails. She might have been considered attractive if she took the trouble. At least that's what Paris had said when she met her at Chief Mike's birthday party. Paris described a few services that she thought would make the transformation, including coloring her roots, cutting off a few inches of split ends and dividing her eyebrows so that she actually had two instead of one. However, my imagination didn't extend that far.

I nodded at J-Rod, a nickname she had picked up because of her prowess on the department's softball team, and sat down in the one remaining chair.

"Detective Rodriguez tells me you brought some pills to be checked out by the lab."

Knowing that J-Rod worked in Vice, I had a sinking feeling about the pills Chris gave me. "One of my sources got them at a party. I was curious. What's the problem? It's Ecstasy, right?"

"Wrong," J-Rod said. "Those pills aren't Ecstasy. It's PMA...or the Superman pill." She waited, but it's been a while since I had worked Vice. She must have noticed the blank look on my face. "PMA, or para-methoxyamphetamine, and its close relative PMMA are extremely dangerous, and if that's being floated around St. Joe, then I need to know."

"Why is it so dangerous?"

J-Rod went into teaching mode. "PMA is significantly more toxic than Ecstasy and ten times more potent. It works more slowly than Ecstasy, so users think the pill didn't work because they're not getting high fast enough, so they take more. When the effects kick in around two hours later, it's too late. They've overdosed. Lastly, scientists believe PMA blocks the brain's enzymes that offset the desired effects of serotonin and dopamine. The brain can't compensate for the increase in serotonin, so users can develop serotonin syndrome."

"What does that do?"

"There are various levels. It can range from agitation and restlessness to seizures, renal failure, coma and death."

I could feel my heart racing, and I took deep breaths in an attempt to slow it down. I reminded myself that Chris hadn't taken the pills, so he was okay, but I couldn't keep my brain from thinking what might have happened. "Any idea where it's coming from?"

"I was hoping you could tell me."

My mind scattered into a million directions. *Do I tell them I got the pills from Mike Maxwell's house? If I do, will I have to tell them about Chris? If they arrest Maxwell, will he be able to figure out that Chris gave me the pills? What if I don't tell them?* The fact that I could lose my job was the least of my worries. The fact that a lot of people could be hurt and possibly lose their life was something that I couldn't live with. There really was no choice. I told them about Mike Maxwell. I told them about the party he had at his house. I told them I knew someone who was there and that they were given the pills while at his house.

Chief Mike looked like he was going to explode. "When exactly were you planning to tell me?"

"I just got the pills this morning. I took them to the lab for analysis. No point in sending a Vice squad until we knew for sure what they were."

J-Rod stood up and rubbed her hands together. "This is better than I hoped. You have someone who's infiltrated Mike Maxwell's organization. That's amazing. We've been trying to get someone close to him for years." She turned to me. "Who is it?"

This was the question I dreaded. I was willing to give them everything I had on Mike Maxwell, especially if he were dealing drugs, but I couldn't give them Chris's name. "It's not an undercover cop. It's…just a source, and I can't take a chance on a leak."

Surprisingly, she accepted it. She leaned close and

lowered her voice. "You think there's a leak on the force?"

I shrugged.

She hopped up and paced. "I hate to admit it, but you might be right. I mean, we've never been able to catch Maxwell. Someone must have been warning him before we searched his places because they were always spick and span." She turned to Chief Mike. "I thought we eliminated that when we got rid of Leonard."

Chief Mike gave me a sideways glance. He scowled. He was either trying to telepathically convey that I wasn't in the inner circle and therefore not privy to these details or he was extremely constipated. Regardless, Detective Rodriguez was beyond noticing.

"I wish you had told me about your source sooner, but I completely understand." She paced. "We need to get these pills off the street as soon as possible. We'll need to coordinate our efforts." She glanced at her watch. "I've got a meeting with the mayor's drug task force. I was going to tell them about the PMA infiltration, but perhaps you'd prefer to come."

My brain started to flash, and I realized a strategy that might work. "No, I'm actually working a homicide. However, could we keep this quiet for a couple more days? I mean, we really don't know how far up the leak goes, and I'd hate for Maxwell to close his operation before you have a chance to make your arrest."

"Sweet Mary Mother of God. You don't think someone on the mayor's task force could possibly be…heaven forbid."

"I just think it's best to keep our cards close to our chest until we're ready to pounce."

"Good idea. Good idea. Well, I have to go to the meeting and tell them something...maybe I can tell them there's been a report of PMA in our area, so we want everyone to be on the lookout." She looked from Chief Mike to me. "I just want you to know that when this is all over, I intend to make sure the mayor recognizes you both for your role in bringing down a dangerous threat to our community, and I expect to have you both standing right there with me at the press conference."

I forced a smile and excused myself before Chief Mike got a chance to grill me. However, the look in his eyes told me he knew what I was doing and that my grilling would be delayed.

I didn't bother to stop at my desk. Instead, I hurried out of the building. If the pills Chris Green had given me were as dangerous as Detective Rodriguez indicated, then Chris might be in more danger now than ever before.

EIGHTEEN

I SPED OUT of the parking lot and used voice commands to dial Chris. Indiana, like most other states in the country, was now "hands free." My phone was secure in its dashboard holder, leaving both of my hands free to steer. Part of my subconscious mind always drifted to the accident that had forever changed my life, which could have been avoided if the sixteen-year-old who had been texting while driving had a similar device. I forced the thought back down to the depths of my subconscious and hurried to the school.

Several tries and all I got was his voicemail telling me to leave a message. My gut contracted into knots. I checked the time and realized that he should be home. I prayed he was. I raced to his house. I pulled up to the curb and hopped out, not bothering to turn off the ignition. I raced up the steps.

Sister Green opened the door with a smile that froze when she looked at my face. "Dear Lord, don't tell me something happened to my boy."

"No, I'm sorry. I didn't mean to frighten you." I smiled to ease the fear I saw on her face. "Chris is fine. I just need to talk to him. That's all. Do you know where he is?"

She patted her chest in an attempt to slow her heart and blew out a long breath. "He's *supposed* to be at the church at choir practice." She gazed into my eyes. "Are you sure he's not in some kind of trouble?"

"I promise you. I just need to talk to him. That's all." I forced myself to stay calm and look normal, but Sister Green, like Mama B, had a sixth sense. Somehow, some way, these mothers could tell when someone was lying. Whatever I did must have worked. She dropped her gaze.

I repeated *Walk don't run* over in my head until I was in the car. Once inside, I looked up and waved before slowly pulling away from the curb. When I was sure I was out of sight, I put the pedal to the metal and made my way to First Baptist Church.

The FBC community is a tight-knit group, which meant anything out of the ordinary would make its way back to Sister Green and Mama B in record time. So, I took several deep breaths and steadied my nerves. This time, I parked and turned off the engine and casually made my way up the steps.

Since our last choir director was murdered, Paris had been helping with the children's and young adult choirs, so it wasn't a surprise when I saw her teaching a new song. Paris had her back to the door, but she turned to look when several of the kids waved when I walked through the doors.

The pastor, Reverend Hilton V. Hamilton, was sitting near the back listening to the rehearsal. He smiled. "RJ, good to see you." He extended his hand.

I shook. "Hello, Reverend."

"What brings you out on this fine evening?" He smiled. "Waiting for our lovely Sister Williams?"

"Actually, I was hoping to have a few words with Chris Green."

He frowned. "He's not in any trouble, is he? Sister Green would be really upset—"

I waved away his concerns. "Not at all. Chris has been helping me with something, and I just have a couple of questions."

I didn't think it was possible, but his gaze was even more intense than Sister Green's and Mama B's. When I was a kid, I used to be terrified of him. Here was a man who talked to Almighty God. The very thought that God could tell him my innermost secrets was enough to scare me straight. It was only later when I was old enough to develop my own personal relationship with God that I realized just because He could tell my secrets didn't mean He would. "If your questions aren't urgent, they should be done in fifteen minutes."

Seeing Chris in the choir took a small amount of my fear away. We locked eyes, and I mouthed that we needed to talk. He nodded, and I relaxed. I turned to Reverend Hamilton. "Sure, I can wait." I sat down on the pew next to him.

We sat in silence for a few minutes and listened to the rehearsal. Reverend Hamilton leaned forward with his arms on the pew in front of him and stared at the choir with a huge smile on his face. Without turning, he said, "Anything bothering you?"

I should have known that nothing slipped past him. I wanted to lie. I wanted to tell him that all was well but lying to a man of God in church was more than I could manage. Suddenly, the weight of everything was more than I could bear. "Can we talk?"

Reverend Hamilton rose. He waved at the kids and headed out the door into the vestibule and downstairs.

I followed.

Reverend Hamilton lived next door to the church, which is where his main office was located. However, he also had a small office in the church basement, which is where he went. They had sectioned off an alcove and closed it off with a sliding glass door. The room held a desk and a couple of chairs. It provided a somewhat quiet place for him to regroup between services.

I followed him inside, and he closed the sliding door behind us. He sat and leaned back in his chair and waited.

I thought it would be difficult to start, but before I knew it, I had unburdened everything to him. I told him about what Chris had seen the night Jake Harrison was murdered. I told him about the party, and I told him about the pills that Chris had given me. He listened in silence, occasionally mumbling *Mercy* or *Dear God*. When I finished, he took a moment to absorb everything and then said, "I can understand why you're nervous, but what are you going to do?"

"I don't know. I need to talk to Chris."

"If he gave you the pills, what's really bothering you?"

"I'm afraid that he may not have given me all of them. What if he kept one or more back?"

"Lord have mercy." His eyes got big, but then he closed them and sat. After a few moments, a smile spread across his face. "Only one person can answer that question, but I do know who we can call on for help." He reached out his hands.

In the small office, we held hands, bowed our heads, closed our eyes and prayed. Reverend Hamilton prayed for protection for both Chris and for me. Then, he asked for wisdom and quoted one of my favorite scriptures, James 1:5: *"If any of you lack wisdom, let him ask of God, that giveth to all men liberally, and upbraideth not; and it shall be given him."* I'd recited that verse many times, especially during my freshman year of college when biology was kicking my butt.

By the time he finished praying, I felt my shoulders drop a bit. I heard the stampede as kids ran downstairs and the laughter and voices as others hurried outside.

Chris came downstairs and stuck his head around the corner. "You need me?"

Reverend Hamilton and I shook hands and said our goodbyes.

Chris glanced nervously at me. "Something wrong?"

"Let's wait until we get in the car."

He nodded but kept looking at me out of the corner of his eyes.

Upstairs, I wasn't surprised to see Paris waiting for me in the vestibule. I tossed my keys to Chris. "Wait for me in the car."

He caught them and practically skipped outside.

Paris smiled. "Apparently, you didn't come to see me."

I held her close and took a deep breath to take in her perfume. I whispered in her ear. "I need to talk to Chris, but I'd love to talk with you later."

"I'd like that." She reached up and kissed me.

Several of the younger girls from the choir chanted, "Ooooh, Sister Williams and RJ sitting in a tree." They broke into laughter.

Paris and I separated. She turned to deal with her giggling youngsters, and I headed down the stairs to my car. When I got to the driver's door, I saw Chris sitting behind the wheel.

He grinned up at me. "Hey, maybe I should drive?"

I held the door open. "Maybe you should leave the driving to someone with a driver's license."

"How am I ever going to learn if nobody teaches me? Granny don't drive and doesn't even have a car. Come on, RJ?"

"I'll teach you to drive." His face lit up. "But not today."

Just as quickly as the light went on, it went out.

"Now, move over," I said. "We need to talk."

He got out and ran around the back to the passenger's door and got in.

Once we were both in the car and strapped in, I took off. I drove in silence for several moments and then asked a question I already knew the answer to: "You hungry?"

"Yeah."

I drove to a local fast food joint that was known more for ice cream than food. However, locals knew that the burgers were as tasty as the milkshakes. The restaurant had an old-fashioned décor and offered indoor dining as well as drive-ins, where the orders were taken over a speaker and delivered by a "car hop." I pulled up to the speaker, and we ordered burgers, onion rings and milkshakes. When the car-hop, who was dressed in a

1950s uniform, delivered the food, we took a few minutes and ate before talking.

Once I felt the edge was off and Chris started to slow down, I said, "Chris, I need to ask you something, and I need you to be one hundred percent honest."

"Okay."

"It's critical that you tell me the truth, and regardless of what you say, I promise I won't get mad and you won't get in trouble." I waited for his nod. When it came, I continued. "Those pills you got at Mike Maxwell's house, did you give me all of them?"

He took a bite of his burger.

"Because I had them analyzed, and those pills are very dangerous."

His eyes got large. He chewed, and eventually he reached in his pocket and pulled out a tissue.

I unwrapped the tissue and inside were two of the pink pills with the Superman "S" stamped on them, just like the others he'd given me. I breathed a sigh of relief.

"How'd you know?" he said.

I thought about his question for a few moments, and then I smiled. "I knew because I was sixteen once too. I know what it's like to be curious."

"I hadn't decided if I was going to try it or not. I mean, my granny really would have killed me if she knew I even thought about it, but… I thought it might make me seem cool if some of the other kids saw me with it, that's all." He looked down.

"Chris, I can tell you to avoid drugs until I'm blue in the face, but ultimately it's your choice. Life is about choices. Where you are and what happens to you is all due to the choices you make each and every day." I

took a deep breath and hoped the wisdom that Reverend Hamilton had prayed for would come. "I remember your mom, Angel. She was pretty and used to wear
these long braids." I glanced over to make sure he was
okay. He ate slowly, but he was listening. "Angel used to
sing in the choir too. She had a nice voice. She wanted
to be a singer."

"I know." He chewed. "Granny told me."

"She was really talented, but she started taking
drugs, and she changed. Her personality changed. She
stopped taking care of herself, and her looks changed.
Even her voice changed."

"Then she moved away and got pregnant with me."

"She did, but she wasn't able to take care of you. Fortunately, she loved you enough to want you to be taken
care of, so she called your grandmother."

Chris glanced out the window.

"Your grandmother went and got you, and she raised
you. She loves you so much. She may be hard on you
sometimes, but that's because she wants more for you.
She wants you to graduate from high school and go to
college. You know, you'd be the first person in your family to do that."

"Really? Granny didn't graduate from high school?"

I shook my head. "Your grandmother didn't have
the opportunities that you have. She had to work in
the fields and take care of her brothers and sisters. You
should ask her about it sometime."

"Wow, I didn't know that."

I chuckled. "I didn't either until a few days ago, but
I know she wants more for you. She wants you to have
chances that she didn't have. Drugs will mess that up.

These pills are dangerous." I took a few minutes and tried to explain some of what I'd learned earlier. I think it must have worked because he stared with his mouth open.

"That's bad," he said. "People could die… I mean, not just over years but one time…they could actually die."

"That's why it's important that we get these off the street. I'm a cop, and I would love to get all drugs off the street, but this is different. Somebody deliberately manufactured something that could harm a lot of people. We need to stop them."

"What do you need from me?"

"I need to know who gave you the pills. Was it Mike Maxwell?"

He thought for quite a while. Eventually, he started to talk. "Mr. Maxwell said he had a gift for me. I thought he was going to give me some money, but he had me follow him to his office. We went downstairs and down a hallway. He had one of the rooms set up like an office. We went in there, and he closed the door. He opened a closet, and there was a huge safe." He hesitated, but after a few seconds, he kept talking. "He opened the safe, and he had a gun and lots of papers and some metal boxes. He took one of the boxes out and opened it. Inside, he had the pills. He poured some in my hand. He said, 'These were for me and my friends. A few of these and you could do anything.'"

I could feel my hands tensing with anger, and I had to force myself to regulate my breathing to keep from hitting something. When I had myself under control, I asked, "What happened next?"

"I took the pills and put them in my pocket. I told

him I'd save them for when I was with my friends. He laughed and gave me two more. He said, 'These are just for you.'"

I had finished my milkshake and was gripping the steering wheel so tight my knuckles had turned white, which wasn't an easy task for a Black man. When I thought I could speak without swearing, I said, "Mike Maxwell is someone who will do anything to make money. He doesn't care who gets hurt as long as he can make a profit."

"Do you think he knows about the bad stuff in those pills?"

"I'm sure he does."

"Man, that's bad. I mean, someone could have been hurt…like my mom. Why doesn't someone stop him? You're a cop. Why don't you stop him?"

"It's not that easy. We've tried to stop him, many times, but…people are scared. No one wants to testify against him. He gets an attorney who gets him off the hook, and then he's back out on the street again, but we aren't giving up. We keep plugging away, and eventually he'll make a mistake and we'll catch him."

Chris's cell phone went off. "This is Granny. I better take it."

I placed our empty containers onto the tray that connected to the microphone and hung over my window, put the car in gear and backed out. I listened while he explained to his grandmother that he was with me and that we were on our way back now. He hung up and was quiet for the remainder of the ride.

I pulled in front of the house, but Chris didn't budge.

He merely sat with his head down. Eventually, he turned to me. "I wanna help."

"You are helping. You—"

"No. I want to help put Mr. Maxwell away. I don't want anyone else to get hurt like my mom. I want to testify."

"You don't have to do this. I shouldn't have told you about the Superman pills. Your grandmother—"

"Raised me to do the right thing. Testifying against someone who gives drugs to kids is the right thing to do. I know that, but..."

"But what?"

"Would you help me explain it to my grandmother?"

NINETEEN

I SPENT TEN minutes trying to talk Chris out of giving an official statement, but once he made up his mind, he was like the lyrics in the old negro spiritual, "Like a Tree Planted By the Water". He would not be moved.

I expected Sister Green would help me convince him to rethink this. However, imagine my surprise when she supported his decision. Again, I tried to explain the danger, but she pursed her lips and set her face like flint. At the end of two hours, neither I, Mama B, Reverend Hamilton, Sister Young or two other women from the Mother's Board were able to change their minds. In fact, if anything, I'd felt as though I'd just stirred up a hornet's nest. Just when I thought I was beyond the point where anything else could shock me, Sister Green went into her bedroom and came back with a shotgun.

"This here was my Papa's gun. Lord, when I moved away from the South, I never thought I'd see the day when I needed it." Sister Green pulled a box of buckshot from her pocket and loaded her weapon.

"Sister Green, please listen to me," I said. "If you're determined to follow through with this, then please allow the police to do our jobs. I will ask to increase the patrols around your house and make sure that Chris is always watched." I could tell by the set of her face that I was talking to a brick wall. "Do you even know how to shoot that?"

She glared at me. "Boy, I was shooting squirrels, rabbits, coons and whatever I could find to put food on the table before you were born."

"Do you have a license?"

That's when I must have crossed the line. She put her hand on her hip and pointed her finger at me. "Now, I'm not big on guns, but I know my second amendment rights, and I pity the fool who would try to take my shotgun." She glared as though I was the fool.

I held up my hands in surrender. "I just don't want a shootout because I guarantee you, if it comes to that, Mike Maxwell will have more firepower."

However, my words fell on death ears. The Mother's Board was organizing a prayer vigil and signing up for guard duty.

I glanced over at Reverend Hamilton, who held up his hands and shook his head in disbelief. I suspect he was as surprised as I was to learn that practically every member of the Mother's Board owned a gun of some type and claimed to know how to use it. When Mama B signed up for guard duty, I nearly passed out. "Wait, you have a gun?"

"Baby, I have several, and before you ask, yes, I have a license and, yes, I know how to use all of them. I used to be a pretty good shot too." She threw her head back and laughed.

By the time I left, I felt like my entire world had been flipped upside down. People I'd known my entire life had shown me a side of themselves that I didn't realize existed. I had promised to increase the patrols around the house, but I was afraid if anyone paused on that street more than five seconds, we were going to have a shootout that would rival the gunfight at the O.K. Corral.

I drove Mama B the short distance to her house. Inside, I asked to see her gun collection.

She went to her bedroom and came out with a shotgun and two pistols. They were old but had been cleaned and well taken care of.

She flopped down into her recliner and turned on the television.

I tried one last ditch effort to talk sense into her. "You know, this isn't like one of your 1970s sitcoms. These people are serious."

"Baby, I know you mean well, but you're young." She rocked. "We've dealt with a lot worse than this Mike Maxwell could ever dish out. We've lived through segregation, Jim Crow, police brutality, fire hoses, dogs, billy clubs and more evil than you will ever know. We may not be young, but don't underestimate us."

"I just don't want anything to happen to you…any of you."

She smiled. "Only the Good Lord can prevent that. If you don't stand up for right…then what's the point? Seems like Black folks been fighting our whole lives. If it ain't slavery, then it's lynch mobs, war…way I see it, this Mike Maxwell is just another fight."

"Aren't you scared?"

"Scared of what?"

"Dying?"

"Nah, I know where I'm going when I leave this earth. If anyone should be scared, it's this Maxwell."

She looked at me and grinned. "Because if Sister Green catches him alone, she's going to beat the tarnation out of him, chop him up in little pieces and make a stew out of him."

She held my gaze for a moment but must have noticed the stricken look on my face because she burst out laughing.

We talked a bit longer, but then I left with a pecan pie. I had a lot to think about.

TWENTY

I CALLED CHIEF MIKE and gave him a quick rundown on the situation, minus my gun-toting church family. He agreed to increase the patrols around the Greens' house and scheduled a meeting for Saturday morning.

I stopped by Paris's house and shared what I could. She laughed until tears ran from her eyes when I told her about the rifle brigade rallying their strength at Sister Green's house.

She wiped away the tears. "I suppose Mama B's right. All of those older women grew up in rural areas where they had to learn to hunt, and they used guns a lot more than someone living in an urban area like St. Joseph."

"I guess, but most of them haven't lived in a rural area for more than forty years. Why do they still have rifles?"

The next day, things moved quickly.

I had arranged to meet Harley early, but I was surprised that he beat me to the precinct.

I updated him on the situation with Chris, and he sat silent for the entire explanation. When I was done, he stared in disbelieve for several seconds. "The Oracle has a gun?"

"She and the rest of those Bible-toting, God-fearing women have an arsenal."

He shook his head. "You think you know people."

Once Harley was up-to-date on my news, he filled me in on what he'd discovered.

The Concierge at Bruce Leonard's condo not only confirmed having seen the couple, but he remembered the date. Apparently, Leonard, normally standoffish and gruff, was extremely talkative and friendly. In fact, he spent several minutes talking to the concierge about MACU's game. "Since I was there," Harley said, "I asked about the security cameras."

"Let me guess, he never left the building."

"We have no way of knowing. The cameras broke and didn't record anything more than static the rest of the night."

"Convenient. We can't prove he left the building, but we can't prove he didn't either. Let's get a warrant for the security footage anyway. My money says our geeks our smarter than Bruce Leonard. They may be able to pull something off them."

I picked up the phone to call the district attorney but put it down when Tim Austen, the assistant D.A., walked over. "Just the man I've been looking for."

"I was going to say the same thing." He yawned. "It's way too early for this, but we've been summoned to a meeting at Mayor Longbow's office."

"Maybe we can kill two birds with one stone."

As we walked over to Mayor Longbow's office, Harley and I explained the evidence we had and the warrants we needed.

When we got to the mayor's office, Tim held up his hands. "Uncle. You two are brutal. I haven't had nearly enough coffee for this."

Harley left and hurried back to get the ball rolling on the warrants, while Tim and I knocked on the mayor's door.

"Enter."

Mayor Longbow, Chief Mike and Detective Rodriguez were sitting at the mayor's conference table, drinking coffee.

Someone had thoughtfully left a carafe of coffee and a box of donuts on the table. Tim's face lit up at the sight of the coffee, and he made a beeline for the carafe.

Chief Mike had given Detective Rodriguez a high-level overview of the case, and I filled in the gaps. Mayor Longbow leaned back in his chair and listened. He was dressed casually and looked ready to hit the golf course. "This Superman pill could cause a lot of damage. I'd love to get this stuff off the street." He didn't say before the elections, but I mentally tacked it on the end of his sentence anyway.

Detective Rodriguez wanted to know how many pills Chris had seen in the safe, but I didn't have that answer. However, I'd arranged for Chris and Mrs. Green to meet me at the precinct later today.

"I'd like to be there when you talk to the witness," Detective Rodriguez said.

I knew that was coming, and I nodded.

Tim Austen downed two cups of coffee quickly. Fully caffeinated, the muscles in his forehead relaxed, and he no longer looked like a junkie in desperate need of his next fix. "Your witness…how reliable is he?"

"He's reliable, but…he's only sixteen."

"Mike Maxwell will have a string of high-powered

attorneys who will make minced meat of him on the witness stand."

I tried to stop my lips, but they were determined to smile. "Maxwell's attorney's may be the least of your problems."

Tim blinked several times and waited.

I explained that Chris Green's grandmother had rallied the elderly women of the church and that they were armed and dangerous.

"Are you joking?" Chief Mike said, turning purple. "The last thing we need is a lot of nervous old women with shotguns meting out vigilante justice on the streets of St. Joseph, no matter how good intentioned."

Mayor Longbow waved down Chief Mike's objections. "I understand your concern, Chief, but I trust Detective Franklin will be able to get the local pastors and the churches help in keeping the women from doing anything…crazy." He stood up, and in that one gesture, our meeting was over.

By the time I made my way back to the precinct, Harley had secured the warrants, and we were off.

First stop, Bruce Leonard.

TWENTY-ONE

BRUCE LEONARD WAS HOME, which made the experience of arresting him even more pleasant. Oh, the look on his face when he was served with his search and arrest warrants.

Leonard didn't take kindly to being handcuffed and paraded through the lobby of his high-rise complex. His normally stone-faced cool was broken, and his face was purple with rage. He sputtered and spewed curses and threats and eventually clammed up and refused to speak without his lawyer.

The search team bagged everything that might remotely be considered useful and fell within the parameters of the warrant. We managed to snag a few bottles of beer, and the production code was the same as the one from our crime scene, which gave me a small thrill. In addition, the team found several bottles of pills. The ones in the medicine cabinet were probably not going to help us, but when we found a bottle hidden under the mattress, well…that just got a cop's blood rushing. Why would anyone need to hide a bottle under a mattress?

In another two-birds-one-stone moment, I executed the warrant for the security footage while at Leonard's complex. I brought along one of our technology geeks.

V. M. BURNS 233

Maureen Morgan was a large African-American woman with a heavy Caribbean accent, which she could turn on and off whenever she wanted but chose not to when talking to me. "RJ, wah gwaan?"

I'd worked with Maureen several times and had gotten a crash course in Jamaican-speak, so I knew the correct response to *What's going on*. "Mi de yah, yuh know."

She laughed. "Ah, you been practicing. Very good, but you need to say it faster, like one word."

Long ago, I had stopped trying to figure out precisely what each word meant when Maureen spoke. Mostly, I replayed the phrases in my mind in slow motion, or I just tried to guess the meaning based on context. "You going to be able to get something off that tape?"

She spent two minutes talking a combination of Jamaican and techno-speak. She must have been able to tell from the glazed look in my eyes that I had no clue what she was talking about.

"I'm going to take that as a yes."

She smiled. "Yah mon. Imma have it perfectly, inna di morrows."

Thirty seconds after she left, I figured out she would have it in the morning. Maureen was good, and she was fast. Chances were she'd have it tonight, but I knew better than to push her. She did not like being pushed.

Since we didn't want to risk Carolyn Harrison destroying any evidence she may have had, while I served the warrant on Bruce Leonard, Harley did the same with the widow.

Back at the precinct, we made sure that both Bruce and Carolyn saw each other, but we kept them separated to prevent collusion.

Since Leonard wouldn't talk without his lawyer, I didn't bother wasting my time questioning him and left him to stew.

I got a call to come to the reception desk. I wasn't surprised to see Chris, Sister Green and Reverend Hamilton. I was expecting them. What I wasn't expecting was the entire senior choir, Mother's Board and Missionary Society to tag along. There were close to thirty women, including Mama B, in the lobby of the precinct.

"What's going on?" I said. "Chris isn't under arrest. He's just giving a statement."

Reverend Hamilton shook his head. "I tried to explain that to them, but they insisted that they all wanted to come."

"Well, they can't just stay here. They're blocking the entrance. Can't you convince them to wait at the church? I promise, Chris will be fine."

Reverend Hamilton turned and addressed his congregation. "Brother Franklin has asked that we not block the entrance. We know everything should be done *decently and in order*, so we are going to honor his request." There was a slight rumble, but no one could argue with the Biblical reference. "Now, Sister Green, Chris and I are going to go give a statement, and I'm asking if the rest of you would wait at the church."

That was apparently asking too much. The rumble grew to a roar. Behind me, I saw a crowd of police had gathered, unsure if they were going to be needed for riot duty.

Sister Young stepped forward. "With all due respect, Reverend, we aren't leaving Chris here alone. However, if it's okay with RJ, then we'll just wait outside on the lawn. We ain't here to cause no trouble, but we ain't leaving until Chris leaves."

I glanced back and caught Chief Mike's eye. He gave a slight nod, and I gave the women a bigger one, letting them know it was okay for them to wait outside. The women filed out of the door quietly, and I made my way to Mama B.

"Really? Et tu?"

Mama B smiled. "I ate before I left home, but I could use a chair."

I gave her a kiss and arranged for a few folding chairs to be placed outside so that some of the women could sit while they waited.

I led Chris, Reverend Hamilton and Sister Green down the hallway to a conference room. On the way, we passed Mike Maxwell and two men in expensive dark suits.

Maxwell glared at me. "What's this all about, Detective? You have no right to—" He caught sight of Chris, and for a moment he stuttered. He quickly regained his equilibrium. He sneered. "I don't know what you think you have on me, Detective, but you won't be able to make anything stick." His eyes narrowed, and like a snake he glared at Chris, who was doing his best to look at anything except Mike Maxwell. However, after a few moments, he looked up and locked eyes with Maxwell.

To my amazement, Chris held the look without wavering.

For a split second, Maxwell was stunned, but he quickly recovered. He glared at Chris. "Boy, you don't want to mess with me. I'm out of your league."

My blood boiled, and I started toward Maxwell. However, I wasn't fast enough. Before I could wrap my hands around his throat, Sister Green shoved me aside and stood nose to nose with him.

"You lay one hand on my boy, and as God is my witness, I'll reach my hand down your throat and rip out your intestines and fry 'em and eat 'em while you watch."

Something in Sister Green's tone sent a shiver down my spine. She meant every word.

Mike Maxwell shuddered and fear flashed across his face. He quickly shook it off and glared back, but it was too late.

I shook off the shock, regained control and ushered Chris, Sister Green and Reverend Hamilton into the conference room, where Tim Austen, Detective Rodriguez and Chief Mike were waiting.

Keeping these two parties from ripping each other apart was turning into one heck of a struggle, and I needed reinforcements. I turned to the only place I knew and prayed.

TWENTY-TWO

CHRIS'S STATEMENT TO the assistant D.A., Detective Rodriguez and Chief Mike was the same as it had been to
me. Detective Rodriguez asked him to describe the pills,
and he did, multiple times. After an hour, Detective
Rodriguez stepped outside and made a phone call. She
had her search warrant and directed her team.

One of the suits who had accompanied Mike Maxwell knocked on the door and requested an audience.
Chief Mike waved him in.

"Look, I think if we could just all sit down together,
we could probably come to some kind of agreement,"
the man said. "Obviously, the boy *believes* he saw something incriminating, but you have no proof. Right now,
you've got the word of a sixteen-year-old kid against an
upstanding member of St. Joseph society." He droned
on but finally finished with, "Either arrest my client or
let him go."

Before I could speak, Chris sat up. "I don't just *believe* I saw him with those pills. I saw it."

The Suit chuckled and gave him a look that screamed,
You poor deluded child. "In a court, you need proof, not
hearsay," he said in a voice that would have been better
suited to a toddler than a teenager.

Chris sat up. "I have proof."

That froze a smirk on The Suit's face. "Really? What proof?"

Chris pulled out the cell phone I had given him. He made a few swipes, adjusted the volume and then held up the phone so that The Suit could see.

Playing on the cell phone was a video of Mike Maxwell opening the safe and pulling out a box full of pink pills with a Superman emblem. Maxwell grinned and said, "These are on the house."

TWENTY-THREE

EVERY ADULT IN that room stared in shock. The suit flushed, turned and walked out.

I'd known Chief Mike for a long time and never had I seen him shocked silent. He stared from Chris to me. "He recorded it? How?"

I turned to Chris, just as stunned as the Chief. "How did you manage to record that? Didn't he see the cell phone?"

Chris held up his wrist. He had an Apple Watch strapped to it. "I connected my Apple Watch to the iPhone you gave me. I just—"

"RJ, get one of our geeks in here," Chief Mike said.

I picked up my cell. After a few minutes, Maureen Morgan tapped on the door and entered.

She glanced at Chief Mike and smiled. She turned down her Jamaican accent and asked, "How can I help you?"

"Watch this. We may need your help if this goes to trial."

Maureen sat down and watched.

Chris propped the iPhone so we could see. He then tapped the watch. "You have to start the camera app from your watch and let it launch the camera app on the phone."

We all huddled around him and watched as the iPhone suddenly displayed the same thing that was on his watch. "Once the camera opens on your phone, you just gotta swipe over to video mode and the remote shutter button on my watch will start the recording." He tapped, waved his watch around the room to get all of our faces and then tapped to stop the recording. He then played the video that was now on his iPhone.

Maureen smiled. "Cool. I knew you could record audio and capture still photos, but I didn't know you could get videos." She looked at Chris. "Is that new?"

Chris shrugged. "Probably came out in one of the latest releases."

"Didn't Mike Maxwell notice all this recording and tapping going on?" Chief Mike asked.

"Nope," Chris said. "Most old folks…uh, I mean adults are used to kids with iPhones and watches and other gadgets." He gave a sideways glance toward his grandmother. "And kids have gotten pretty good at doing stuff on the down low so we don't get in trouble in school."

Sister Green frowned but remained silent.

There was another tap on the door. The suit opened the door and beckoned for Tim to come out.

Tim stood up and whispered, "I think Mr. Maxwell might be looking for a deal." He smiled as he left the room.

Detective J-Rod beamed. "I better go and update the mayor. I can't believe we nailed the son-of-a-b—" She glanced at Reverend Hamilton and swallowed the rest of it. She and Chief Mike left.

Sister Green stared at me. "What happens now?"

"Nothing. You guys might as well go home."

"But what about that man?" she asked. "When do we go to court to testify?"

"I don't think this case will be going to court." I explained that Mike Maxwell's lawyers and the District Attorney's office would most likely negotiate a deal where Maxwell would go to jail for fifteen to twenty years.

"You mean Chris won't have to testify?"

I shook my head. "It doesn't look that way."

"Praise the Lord. Thank you, Jesus." Sister Green rejoiced as tears of joy streamed down her face.

"We will need to hang onto Chris's watch and phone." I turned to Maureen. "That is unless…"

"Give me a few. I'll get everything we need." She gave Chris a smile and picked up the watch and phone and left.

Reverend Hamilton turned to me. "I can't believe this. I expected a long ordeal, but…thanks to you." He pointed up toward the heavens. "And the Good Lord above, y'all worked it all out."

"Reverend, I wish I could take credit for this, but this is beyond what I had hoped or dreamed."

Reverend Hamilton smiled. "This is what I call an Ephesians 3:20 result."

I must have looked confused.

He smiled and quoted: *"Now unto Him that is able to do exceedingly abundantly above all that we ask or think, according to the power that worketh in us."*

Sister Green sat in her chair, crying, rocking and praising God until Maureen returned with Chris's watch and phone. Then, I escorted them outside.

Even before we reached the lobby, I could hear singing. The women outside were singing spirituals. A news crew had arrived, and a crowd of law enforcement and civilians were outside clapping and singing. When Reverend Hamilton, Sister Green and Chris came outside, the crowd erupted. They shouted praises, clapped, sang and rejoiced.

I caught sight of Mama B and walked over. She was sitting on one of the foldup chairs. She too was crying and praising God, so I merely kissed her cheek and left.

My cell phone started ringing before I reached the door. I saw Harley's face and swiped. "What's up?"

"You might want to come. Things are getting ugly in here."

TWENTY-FOUR

WHEN I HURRIED down the hall, I didn't need to guess which room. I merely followed the shouts.

I ran into Harley standing between the two rooms where Carolyn Harrison and Bruce Leonard were sitting. I turned to him. "What the...?"

"All was fine until the lab came back and said the pills found under Leonard's mattress contained Valium." He held up a bag with the bottle of pills and handed me a lab report. "That's when Leonard lost it. He said Carolyn Harrison was framing him for the murder."

I looked at him. "Is his lawyer in there?"

He nodded.

I entered the room where Bruce Leonard was ranting. "It's her. That black widow is setting me up, but I'm not taking the fall." He yelled at the wall separating them, "I'm not going down alone."

"Are you saying you want to make a statement?"

His lawyer was a small man with big glasses that concealed beady eyes. "Mr. Leonard, I don't recommend—"

Bruce turned on him. "You don't recommend? You! I'm a former cop. If I go to jail, I'll be dead in less than a week. I want a deal. You need to make a deal. That's what I'm paying you for."

Beady Eyes looked as though he would have liked to swallow glass, but he merely turned to me. "Perhaps you'd better give us a few moments alone."

We agreed and walked out. While Bruce Leonard bared his soul to his lawyer, we went into the room with Carolyn Harrison.

In contrast to the massive meltdown happening next door, the widow was cool, calm and collected.

"Officers, clearly Bruce Leonard is insane. That man is completely out of control. He must have killed my husband without my knowledge." Her big blue eyes pleaded with us and screamed sincerity.

I sat in one of the chairs across from her. "Mrs. Harrison, I'm confused. You said in your statement that you and Bruce Leonard were together all night. So, I'm not sure how he could have killed your husband without your knowledge?"

Carolyn Harrison had had plenty of time to think up a response to that. In fact, she had likely started to think of a response while her husband was alive. "He must have drugged me, just like he drugged poor Marti. He must have slipped Valium in both of our drinks." She gave me a wide-eyed stare.

"How did you know Marti was drugged with Valium?" Harley asked.

She sighed. "Why, you told me…or someone told me. Maybe it was him." She pointed next door.

"I mentioned that Marti was drugged, but I never said with what."

She waved it away. "Then, it must have been him. He told me what he'd done, but I was terrified. I mean you heard him. He's violent. I was scared. I knew if I said anything, I'd end up just like Jake." She shivered.

I tapped my Apple Watch. "So, you're saying that Bruce Leonard *told* you he drugged Marti Alexander and murdered your husband?"

"Yes, I was terrified. I knew if I didn't go along with his plan, that he'd kill me too." She sobbed.

"Hang on." I tapped my watch, got up and walked out. Harley and I went back into the room with Bruce Leonard and his attorney.

Beady Eyes smiled. "My client was under duress earlier when he said he wanted a deal. He has since had a change of heart and——"

I tapped my watch. Carolyn Harrison's voice stating that Bruce Leonard murdered her husband filled the room. I tapped it. "I'm sorry. I don't know how that happened, I——"

Bruce Leonard shoved his chair back, leapt up and raced to the wall. He pounded on the wall of the room where he knew Carolyn Harrison waited. He beat the wall and screamed obscenities. "You liar. You're trying to frame me for your murder, but it won't work." He turned to me. "She did it. It was all her idea. She came up with the entire plan. She hated Marti. She hated that the entire Harrison clan all thought Marti walked on water and considered her nothing more than a dirty little *gold digger*. It was all her idea. She drugged Marti. When she was knocked out, Carolyn took her shoes, her gun, cell phone and an earring. She waited until we were at the river, and then she called Jake from there so Marti's phone would ping the cell tower. Then, she put on Marti's clothes and shoes——"

"Mr. Leonard, as your attorney, I caution you to—"

"Shut up!" Bruce Leonard was too far gone to listen to counsel now. "You just get me a deal. You get me ten years in one of those cushy low-security country clubs with embezzlers, insider traders and forgers. That's what you do!" He returned to the wall and yelled more obscenities.

"We can't make any deals," I said. "That's up to the D.A."

Bruce Leonard paused from pounding the wall. "Then you get somebody in here who *can make a deal*, because I'm going to sing like a canary and make sure that witch fries like a slab of bacon."

TWENTY-FIVE

IT TOOK HOURS before we were able to leave. Beady Eyes may not have looked tough, but he negotiated a rock-solid deal for his client. Once the deal was made, Leonard kept his word and spilled his guts.

Mayor Longbow asked for an update, so Harley, Chief Mike, J-Rod, Tim Austen and I spent two hours making sure the mayor knew everything we knew. It was late, and none of us had stopped to eat, so the mayor ordered pizza. We sat at the conference table where we had sat earlier that day. Hard to believe it was the same day, but we briefed Mayor Longbow and J-Rod. They had a press conference first thing in the morning, and we needed to make sure they had all the facts.

"RJ, I really think you should attend the press conference." Now that the case was over and we were in an informal atmosphere, Detective Rodriguez must have felt more relaxed than she had earlier, so it was RJ rather than Detective Franklin. "After all, it was all because of you that we were able to finally get Mike Maxwell and remove a very dangerous drug from our streets."

I shook my head. "I'm just a cop. I was doing what the people of St. Joseph pay me to do. That's all."

Tim Austen held up one of the beer bottles the mayor

had taken out of his fridge for us. "I don't think I will ever be able to look at a bottle or can of beer the same way after this case."

Mayor Longbow had been silent for several minutes, and when I glanced up, I felt his eyes looking at me. "Forgive me for staring, Detective, but how did you know?"

"Excuse me?" I asked. "How did I know what?"

"How did you know that Marti Alexander hadn't killed her husband? Carolyn Harrison and Bruce Leonard had done a great job planting evidence to make it look like she was guilty. Nine out of ten officers would have simply arrested her and let the jury do their dirty work. What made you keep digging?"

I wracked my brain for an acceptable answer, but the only thing that came to mind were Mama B's words. "I didn't have peace about it." I stood up and stretched. "Now, if you will all excuse me, I'm pretty tired. I'm going to go home and get some sleep. I've got to get up early for church tomorrow."

* * * * *

Steal away, steal away, steal away to Jesus
Steal away, steal away home
I ain't got long to stay here

My Lord, He calls me
He calls me by the thunder
The trumpet sounds within-a my soul
I ain't got long to stay here

Green trees are bending
Po' sinner stand a-trembling
The trumpet sounds within-a my soul
I ain't got long to stay here

RJ's Favorite Meals

ELVIRA'S CORNBREAD DRESSING

Ingredients:

One small skillet of Jiffy cornbread and one small skillet of cornbread (My mom didn't use Jiffy; this is my sister's addition—if you don't use the Jiffy cornbread, then make a large pan/skillet of cornbread). Make the cornbread a few days ahead and allow it to get stale, then crumble together.
1-2 bags of cornbread stuffing
(we use Pepperidge Farm)
4 stalks of celery finely chopped
3 medium onions finely chopped
1 tablespoon pepper
2 teaspoons dried sage
4 tablespoons of butter
5 eggs (room temperature)
2-3 cans (32 ounces) chicken broth

1. Mix together the crumbled cornbread and stuffing.

2. Boil the turkey neck, giblets, kidneys and heart in the 32 ounces of chicken broth.

3. Take the turkey butt and fat and sauté—when the fat liquifies, add onions and celery to soften—add 4 tablespoons of butter if it gets dry.

4. Add pepper to dry ingredients and mix.

5. Add sage to dry ingredients and mix.

6. Remove large pieces of skin from sautéed vegetables and mix into dry ingredients.

7. Beat eggs and mix into dressing (this should help it stay together).

8. Chop gizzard/heart/liver and mix with dressing* (optional—my mom always did this, but my sister and I don't like gizzards, so my mom always made one pan without it).

9. Cook turkey and pour pan drippings into dressing.

10. Bring two of the 32-ounce cartons of chicken broth to a boil and pour into dressing.

11. When the turkey is done, put the dressing in a pan with the turkey (you can add to the cavity if you want, but we don't)—bake uncovered and let the dressing and the turkey brown at 325 degrees.

MAMA B AND ADRENA'S BANANA PUDDING

Ingredients:

14-ounce can condensed milk
1½ cup cold water
4-ounce box instant pudding
(banana or vanilla)
2 cups (1 pint) heavy whipping cream
3-4 bananas, sliced and dipped in lemon juice
Vanilla wafers

1. Combine condensed milk and water.

2. Add pudding and beat well.

3. Chill for 5 minutes.

4. Whip heavy whipping cream until it peaks, approximately 10–15 minutes.

5. Fold whipped cream into pudding/milk/water mixture until blended.

6. Layer vanilla wafers/bananas, pudding.

7. Chill thoroughly.

SMOTHERED CABBAGE

Ingredients:

1 large head cabbage, cored and sliced
1 large onion, diced
1 3-ounce package of real bacon bits
6 bacon slices, chopped
1 tablespoon salt
1 tablespoon sugar
1 teaspoon pepper
½ teaspoon onion powder
½ teaspoon garlic powder
¼ teaspoon paprika

1. Place the bacon in a large pot and cook over medium-high heat until crispy.

2. Add the onion and cook until caramelized.

3. Stir in the cabbage and continue to cook and stir (10–15 minutes). The cabbage will soften, wilt and cook

down. Season with salt, pepper, onion powder, garlic powder, sugar and paprika. Reduce heat to low, cover and simmer, stirring occasionally for about 30 minutes. Sprinkle bacon bits and mix before serving.

BLACK-EYED PEAS

Ingredients:

1-pound dried black-eyed peas
1 ham hock or smoked turkey wings
¼ cup bacon drippings
½ teaspoon Lowry's Season Salt
¼ teaspoon black pepper
1 large onion, diced
½ teaspoon sugar
*Optional—1 jalapeno seeded and minced

1. Pour the peas into a bowl and pick out anything that shouldn't be there (e.g., small stones, twigs, etc.).

2. Rinse the peas well and let them soak for 30 minutes in cold water.

3. Drain the peas and rinse with cold water.

4. Combine all of the ingredients in a large stockpot.

Cover with enough cold water to cover the peas by an inch. Bring to a boil over high heat.

5. Reduce the heat to simmer. Cover and cook until the peas are tender, about 90 minutes. Add more water if needed and cook to desired level of tenderness (peas should be soft but not mushy).

CANDIED SWEET POTATOES

Ingredients:

*6 medium sweet potatoes, peeled and sliced
(I prefer them thinly sliced, about ¼ inch)
1 teaspoon pure vanilla
4 tablespoon unsalted butter, softened
½ cup granulated sugar
½ cup light brown sugar
1 teaspoon ground cinnamon
1 teaspoon ground nutmeg*

1. Melt butter in a medium pot over medium-low heat.

2. Combine sugar, cinnamon and nutmeg in a small bowl.

3. Add sliced potatoes to melted butter and turn to coat.

4. Sprinkle sugar mixture over potatoes, stir to coat.

5. Cover, reduce heat to low.

6. Stirring occasionally, cook for 50–60 minutes (depending on how thick you sliced your potatoes) or until potatoes are tender.

ELVIRA'S FRIED CHICKEN

Ingredients:

8 pieces of chicken rinsed and patted dry
(I remove the skin, but this is optional)
1 cup all-purpose flour
½ teaspoon Lowry's Season Salt
¼ teaspoon ground black pepper
2 large eggs, beaten
2 tablespoons paprika
Vegetable oil

1. Trim the excess fat and skin from each piece of chicken and pat with a paper towel to make sure it is dry.

2. Beat the eggs in a shallow bowl.

3. Combine the flour, salt, pepper and paprika and place in a paper bag or bowl.

4. Dip the chicken into the egg mixture and then dredge

in the flour and seasoning or place in the bag and shake to coat and shake off excess flour.

5. Pour enough vegetable oil into a cast iron skillet until it covers ⅓ of the sides and heat over high heat until a small bit of flour sizzles.

6. Add a few pieces of chicken to the skillet (be careful, the oil may splatter). Do not overcrowd or the chicken will turn out greasy. Using tongs, turn the chicken until they are golden brown on all sides and cooked through (if pierced with a fork in the thickest part, the chicken should not be pink, and the juices will be clear).

7. Remove the cooked chicken from the skillet and place on paper towels to drain (if you need to cook the chicken in batches, you can keep the fried chicken warm by placing it on a baking sheet and keeping it in the oven at 250 degrees).

8. Sprinkle all of the chicken with paprika and serve hot.

V. M. BURNS (Valerie) was born and raised in South Bend, Indiana. She is the Agatha nominated author of the Mystery Bookshop Mystery Series and The Dog Club Mystery Series. She currently lives in Eastern Tennessee with her poodles.